The Impossible

Return to Innocence

The Impossible

Return to Innocence

Written by

J.D. Clair

MERAKI HOUSE

P U B L I S H I N G

(C) 2016 by J.D. Clair.

Published by **MERAKI HOUSE PUBLISHING INC.**

For any information regarding permission contact
J.D. Clair via **JDCLAIR.COM**

Printed in the United States of America
First publication, 2016.

Paperback ISBN - 978-0-9937996-2-4

eBook ISBN – 978-0-9937996-3-1

Book cover design by
reborn
Design Redefined

DEDICATION

To my supportive parents, my loving wife, my inspiring children, and above all... to my redeeming God, through whom all things are possible.

CONTENTS

Chapter 1:
RUN

All I could do was scream. My blood was on her hands; Fresh, red, and warm; unsure why she hated me.

"Stop." I cried. "Please Mama... Stop!"

My plea raced past deaf ears. She didn't yell. She didn't explain... She only thrashed at me, ignoring the blades of glass that pressed further into her hand, cutting us both as she struck me over and over again.

I used to be her baby. I used to be her angel.... but Mom changed. She's different. She wants me dead... All because I broke the grandfather clock.

I began coughing, struggling to swallow a shallow breath of air past the blood that accumulated in my throat: Gasping to form words.

"I'm... Sorry... It was... an... accident. Please!"

I was only 12 years old.

She was on top of me, the weight of her body too much for me to escape. The pile of glass burrowed in her fist cut my face as she struck me again, and again.

"Please... stop, Mama!" I pleaded.

She cried too though she didn't say anything. No reply. No words. Only broken hearted grunts accompanied by the violent sting of her repeated cuts. Her eyes were far off, as though she was staring through the world. As though she couldn't see me at all. All semblance of humanity vanished from her countenance. She didn't react to anything. Not her pain, and certainly not mine. She didn't say anything. She only kept striking me.

I was scared. I was helpless. She was killing me.

"WHAT THE HELL?" Tony, my older brother, yelled as he opened the front door, finding our struggle within the bloody mess. With only a moment's pause he dove, tackling her off of me, and clasping around her tightly with his arms and legs. She wailed frantically to escape him. Her arms swatted at the air, determined to once again take hold of me and complete the murder she began. I turned to my side, desperate for air, frozen in that inhuman gaze as her eyes fixed on what world lay past me.

"Run, Dominick!" Tony commanded.

I could barely stand, but as she clawed her way to end me, I saw there was only death at the bottom of the broken grandfather clock.

I ran.

Chapter 2:
The Blur

It had been 5 years since my mother almost killed me, and while I learned to live ashamed of that which was beyond my control, I never stopped running.

I was 17, entering into the final months of my junior year in high school. While I was a proud Bronco possessed by school spirit, with a green and white soul, academia had lost its appeal. This winter couldn't end fast enough. For me, summer and fall were the months with the most promise; endless days of cool, soothing air and time to spend doing anything I wanted.

I was plugged into football and track at school and jogged whenever I could between practices; anything to get out of the house. Even the escape of video games lost their appeal after a while. I wanted to be outside doing anything. I wanted to run.

"Where are you going?" my mother asked knowing exactly where I was going. She saw the green high-top training shoes I was lacing up, the shoes I only wear when going for a run.

I didn't respond.

"Where are you going, Dominick?" she asked again in frustration.

"For a jog." I mumbled.

"Did you do your homework?" she asked weakly. She was searching for an excuse to talk to me and I didn't want to give her the satisfaction.

"Did you take your medicine?" I shot back with contempt.

She left the room sobbing, though, I didn't feel bad. Hardly a day goes by that I don't think about when she attacked me. The blood. The glass. The cuts. The event was as ever present in my mind as the soft skin scars that permanently creased my forehead, cheek, and ear. Many of the cuts healed, others faded into jagged pink folds, but the marred hairline gave the appearance I was mauled by a large dog or a bear. At least, that's what I told people brave enough to ask me.

For years I would have nightmares of my mother, walking into my room at night with those cold, distant, inhuman eyes, glowing in the dark blue. She would pull the glass from her nerve damaged hand and stab me in my stomach while I lay asleep in bed and I would wake up terrified. No child should have to hide a knife under their pillow to protect themselves, especially from their mother. My dad would try to reassure me saying 'Your mom was ill. You still need to respect her. She was suffering from a mental disease that caused her to have an episode.'

'An episode'… that's what he thought of it. As if it was the show of the week. I loved my dad, but I never could understand how he could let her live with us after what she did. Especially with my younger sister, Gina, in the house. She should have been in jail, or better yet, in one of those horrible sanitariums that couldn't legally exist anymore, but should for people like her.

I stepped outside in my gray sweats and stretched. The sky was lost in a dense white fog that blended into a still winter morning landscape with faint smells of salt and gas powered snow blowers that hung low in the air. It was nearly spring and this was possibly my last run in the cold season. I bounced on my toes for a few strides, hopping back and forth on the thin layer of crunching snow. It was only cold for the first minute or so. Then, as I began to increase my speed, the tightening and burning of my muscles to the exotic bitter rush of wind took me to a state between pain and euphoria. That place where the mind breaks free of the body and enters the hidden static between worries and responsibilities. I was always most comfortable there... in the blur.

My family, my friends, and the entire world slip away from me while I'm lost in the blur of a run. Brick houses on long stretches of suburban blocks folded into one another as I raced through the streets. The music in my headphones overwhelms the noise of the world until the music, too, fades to obscurity. The world bends around, forming a tunnel, which becomes replaced by imagination. Percussed breath maintains my pace, giving rhythm to my thoughts. I always found myself replaying the events of that horrible day; chasing the phantom echo of history. I felt I could nearly change things, if only I could run faster.

For the next hour, the blur becomes my new world, until I am jolted by an awakening buzz. The alarm shakes aggravated, and like a fishing reel, I am pulled back to consciousness. From there I stumble home, rubber legged, sore, and accomplished.

Chapter 3:
The Threshold

—⁕❀⁂—

The house was empty when I arrived home. I wasn't sure where my mother had gone, but I was glad she wasn't here.

I sat on a stool near the kitchen to pry my green high-tops off my sweat soaked feet when I noticed a large envelope on a table in the living room. Normally I didn't care about the mail, but I was expecting something, and this package had my name on it. My class ring had come in. A quick glance revealed all my pre-selected choices had been met. The ring was white gold with a green stone, and the inscriptions were right.

I was worried that I smudged the paperwork when I erased my first name from the form and put my last name, Adessi, but somehow they read it. I slipped the ring on. It was a little tight due to the swelling in my hands from jogging.

I struggled to get it off when my eyes caught the family photo above the table. There the picture rested for the last 5 years and I hated it more with each passing day. It was the last family photo we'd taken all together.

There we were, all dark haired and bright eyed in forced photographed splendor. Our smiles all looked strained from endless minutes of involuntary false joy. My dad standing tall in the back rested his hand on my shoulder, my older brother Tony, my baby sister Gina, and a pitiful 12-year-old me. I looked awful, even without the disfigured cuts on my face.

I was in the awkward years... my cheeks had plumped up, and early puberty acne had attacked full force. I had a black eye from a fight I had gotten in over something snarky I said. Tony suggested covering the black eye with makeup, but it still showed enough that the photographer decided to use his editing tools to make a big blurred mess out of the right half of my face. Everyone said I'd look back and laugh at it someday. That day hadn't come yet.

What made the picture worse was that Tony looked really good in it. So good that he made sure to pass out a copy to all of his friends. Tony was 2 years older than me and had a wrestler's physique. The girls loved him. We'd go through periods of being thicker than thieves, to somehow becoming strangers. When he went to high school, leaving me in 7th grade, he faded off into popularity. It seemed impossible to find someone who didn't like him. By the time I made it into high school as a freshman, he was a junior, and despite the social barrier generally formed between the upper and lower class students, he took me under his wing. We'd often train together; him for wrestling, me for track... and though I was more slender than Tony, I loved when people would tell me that we looked alike. Tony was my hero. Now he's in college... I miss him.

Gina was a cute little thing; so dainty, and yet unbelievably headstrong. The girl was fearless. Once she climbed up the iron rod support beam on the front porch of our yellow brick house and somehow managed to get onto the garage roof. I swear if I was as reckless with my body as she was I'd be in a full body cast by the end of the week. Now she was 6, in kindergarten, and more opinionated than ever. I worried about her living in this house and sometimes hated how much of a hold she had on me. Gina spent most of her time at Nonna's house a few blocks over. I think we all felt that she was safer there.

Even though I just got home, and the house was empty, I couldn't shake the feeling that my mother would come back soon. I didn't have anywhere to be, but I knew I didn't want to be home when she arrived. I sent my buddy Cody a text saying "What's up?" before jumping in the shower. When I came out, I saw he had replied, "At work."

Cody was a senior who worked for a local coffee company near the mall called the Dark Drip. I'm not a big fan of coffee, but enough sugar and cream could make almost anything taste good. Besides, it was something to do.

"Cool. I'll swing by."

I threw on a green bronco t-shirt, jeans, gray leather jacket, and began lacing up my white high-tops with a green stripe when I heard a cry.

It sounded like a child.

"Gina!" I called out. My mind raced through all the horrible things that could be happening.

I chased the sound to a staircase in the back corner of the house that lead to the attic. The stairs were held together by soft wood, impaled with discolored nails of green and red rust. The stair dipped at first, requiring a few steps down before reaching a miniature platform, taking an angled turn and then resuming steps which stretched high up to the ceiling. I rushed over the irregular stoop, climbing up past an old shelf with chipped paint.

The cries were getting louder.

A few more steps and I was touching the ceiling where a latched horizontal door cut through the staircase. The door was much heavier than I thought it would be. After a few weak pushes didn't fold the hinge inward, I shoved the door with both hands turning it over with a heavy *THUMP*.

"Gina!" I yelled.

The crying stopped, leaving only the sour sound of blowing wind bending the wooden roof into an audible moan above hidden whispers.

"Gina!" I called out again as I climbed up, reaching blindly for a string to turn on the light. A few awkward gropes of the air lead to the string, and a click later the space was visible.

I didn't realize it until then that my fists were clenched white. I panned around the room, unsure of what I'd find. I imagined blood and horror as my little sister had fallen to the fate intended for me all those years ago. There was nothing.

There was no Gina… no blood… no sign of trouble at all. I began to wonder if the desperate cries I heard were real or if my mind was playing tricks on me.

I examined the floor carefully, remembering that it

was merely unfinished beams the ceiling below was fixed to, and only a few places seemed to be stable enough to stand or walk. I looked at the boxes of old nothings, which said "Christmas decorations", "Tony's trophies" and "baby clothes".

I held my breath in silence, hoping for an answer when a whistle caught my ear. The wind was coming in through a window on the far side.

I found some decent footing and made my way over, trying to dodge all the dangling cobwebs. When I reached the far end, the obstruction over the window became more apparent. There was some kind of standing mirror frame facing the window.

I pulled the mirror away and turned it to find the other side was missing the reflective glass. The window, which looked out onto the street, must have somehow opened to a painful wind. Part of me hoped there'd be something more to it, like a better view of the girl down the street's room, or maybe a bird's eye view to something strange, something exciting. All I could see were our neighbors, the Murphys, piling into the car for what I assume was another family vacation. I closed the window and began making my way back towards the stairwell.

I stood above the hole, took one last look in the dim room, and then pulled the string. The light clicked off, but the room was no longer the same pitch of dark as it was when I entered. I stood for a moment looking at the now exposed window thinking that the room looked pretty cool now in the ambient light of the exposed window. I was just about to leave when the whistle of the air returned with an ominous moan. Did the window jarred open again (sainted of jarred), I wondered?

My eyes were fixed on the faint light as I tried to decide whether to fix the window or leave it. I wasn't certain that it was even broken but if it was and my dad found out I was in the attic I knew I'd be responsible somehow. So I again reached for the string again but this time, couldn't find it.

The ambient light began to brighten. My eyes fixated. It almost appeared as though the window had enlarged and continued to grow until it swelled in with a forceful gust of wind. The wind no longer howled or moaned, but instead filled the air with the shaking roar of a turning sea. The noise was violent. It overtook the idle spaces, conquering with deafening madness. Then, the savage rush stole me into a blinding light.

One could hardly determine where the threshold between our world, the real world, was and where this new place had begun. The transition between realities was similar to the moment one realizes they are in a dream; eyes opened and shut simultaneously while being pulled backward, somehow unawake yet fully aware of this remarkable condition; bringing me to this new place which I would learn was called the Furtherland. For the Furtherland was beyond the farthest reaches of a simple world known to man and stretched into an expanse. There, in that expanse, no one can determine where the beginning starts and when the end ceases.

It's near impossible to describe the counterintuitive nature of a disrupted reality; it is not like a circle where the head and the tail continue infinitely into one another. No, this place was as though glass had an image stained into it moments before breaking into incalculable pieces.

These areas, these thresholds where Alice fell into the rabbit hole, where Dorothy soared over the rainbow, or even where Peter Pan passed the second star to the right and straight on till morning; it was these places which transcended sanity and brought a person into madness; where time separated from space. And while The spectacle of shifting between realities was enough to ponder endlessly.   As the glass exploded in a violent twist, the wind stole me in a reckless romance. I was in a bright abyss. Everything Shattered.

My eyes could hardly focus on what was before me. It was a new world; one my brain immediately warred against. I didn't know where I was. I became a traveler, a cosmonaut to the wild, untamed place, granted the opportunity to visit a new uncharted world. I had transcended reality, slipping between the static of the universe on a hidden path to beyond the blur.

Reality was shattered...

Chapter 4:

The Cliff and the

Creatures

—❦—

I was outside, standing atop a large garden of sandy white boulders on a cliff, staring out into a foreign land. I had little to no idea where I'd gone or how I'd gotten there. I gazed astonished at the foreign plane, with all the wonder and adventure of a lost child.

I saw oceans, streams, and long areas of flat land. To one side was a thick gray forest, to the other a strange cut of mountain connected to the cliff I was presently occupying. Beyond that was a long stretch of flat desert land with eerie shaped trees with a notch resembling a head bowed in prayer, and long arms stretched upward in an ominous pose. Nothing was familiar. Nothing felt comforting.

A large cloud in the form of a horse darting was clearly defined in complex detail and alien among the low-hanging sky. The horizon appeared much closer than I'd ever noticed before as if I had somehow made it to the edge of the earth. Was this earth? Had I somehow come to find myself in an alien world, one much smaller than the one I'd left?

The savage rush of wind slowed and faded revealing a tuneful hum, which I scanned to find the source of. At the farthest distance I could see, at what appeared to be the center of the Furtherland, were magnificently massive glass skyscrapers. This cluster of tall jagged crystal towers appeared as if it had been arranged into a city block. It was from here that the hum came. The middle sang a hollow moan, in the way a breath in the neck of a bottle whistles mournfully as it rises out. The air was milky fresh and dense as it emerged from its chambers, taking only a few moments to ignite from pale to rich varying colors. I couldn't help but stare into hypnotic radiance, losing myself for countless minutes.

The wind was on fire.
The wind was alive.

When I finally pulled myself away from the sight of the living wind, I surveyed the vast landscapes that lay below and the only thing I could think to do was call out into the new world.

"HELLO?" I shouted.

"...hello..." A faint echo returned like a haunting whisper, warping the call I made into something hardly resembling my voice to the extent that its tone chilled me to the core; disturbing my awakening soul. I didn't know where I was, but I knew I didn't want to be there.

Suddenly, a creature roughly the size of a small dog crawled up onto the rock. It strongly resembled a blue jay with a soft blue feathery coat that tiled like a mosaic of whites, blues, and blacks towards the longer back feathers. The head had a large crest which began from its black razor sharp beak, past its hollow black marble eyes and crowned him like heavily gelled hair sticking straight up. Its belly was white and it had four black legs, much thicker than any bird I'd ever seen, but still thin and narrow along with the rest of the body. The bird had no wings; however, each feature testified that this creature was incredibly fast. I knew at first blush I couldn't outrun it, especially not on the unbalanced crag of the cliff. So I patronized the animal.

"Nice, bird-dog thing..." I said as soothing as possible. The creature darted up to me in a flash and took a bite at my ankle.

"WHAT THE HELL!" I yelled at the creature, kicking the chalky stone towards it. The creature became startled and scurried off. I felt fortunate to be wearing the high-tops. Even the mere pressure of the beak clenching at my ankle took a moment to wear off.

It was horrifying to be in such a new place, but at least that was one creature I didn't have to worry about. I stumbled around the rocks until I found what appeared to be an opening. I looked in and shouted. No echo returned. No growls or roars returned either. I walked around the cliff edges a little longer before deciding that the opening might be a tunnel that leads to the ground. What I found on the inside was an elaborate cave, where I realized a startling truth...

Light did not require a source to exist here in the Furtherland. Light simply was. There were glowing gems breaking through the walls of the cave. At first I thought such stones must be magical to produce such a beautiful ambiance, until I discovered that light was captured and swayed like water filling a glass, transforming the crystal stones into fluorescent bulbs. The fiery wind I saw erupt from the glass columns filled the cave. The gems seemed incapable of creating light but merely tamed it as though the glowing rocks' mere existence was to ensnare the luminescent air. The light moved as though millions of microscopic specks of dust had suddenly come alive with passion. They were obtainable stars that blazed: never burning, never fizzling, each harboring heavenly movement which became all the more astounding as the light swayed in rhythm to a distant melody.

The cave sank deeper, but the unnatural glow persisted, dancing off the walls, to a joyful song. The voice grew slowly at first, and then as if it rounded a corner grew exponentially louder in a matter of moments. "The world is enchanted, even the walls sing." I thought. That was until I saw the source and the suddenly, as if unable to be viewed directly, the song stopped.

Lumbering through the cave was a large creature. His countenance was heavy, swaying to his own tune in synchronization with the lights, paying no mind to slapping his limbs into crumbling walls as though he was without regard to barriers. Its proportions were odd. The torso was round and firm with fat while the long arms and legs thinned as though they had been stretched with dark chicken-like scales down to his clawed fists.

The beast had short stiff fur on his front except where the scales also covered his chest and stomach areas. His spine was lengthy with lush quills and his head was also bristling with quills but softened around his pointed long-nosed face, resembling the overbite of a shark, but with large fox-like ears. He surely was a monster. Though, there was something so innocent about him. Something so kind in his eyes that the initial fight or flight shock of seeing him dissipated almost immediately. Perhaps it was the creature's slow unbalanced stride that testified to a gentle nature.

"I didn't see you there, big guy. I'm Piop." said the kind creature.

"Hi I'm Dominick." I returned, unsure why the large beast would refer to me as 'big guy'.

"Where are you from, Dominick? You're a strange color. I've never seen one of what you are before. Then again, I don't come over to these parts much too often."

"I'm from... earth?" I didn't mean to give such a hesitant reply, but I wasn't sure if we were still on earth or even if he knew what earth was. Then again, I was talking in English to a monster in a cave in a place called the Furtherland. Little victories.

"Did you get here on your own?" He continued.

"I'm not sure... I just kind of woke up here."

"Well, that is something. It must take an incredibly powerful guy to make it all the way to a new place on accident. I've never been anywhere on accident."

First he calls me big, then powerful. It was hard to not feel flattered, but this beast was at least twice my size and unquestionably more powerful. His weight alone challenged the strength of the solid rock walls which he cracked as he stumbled into them. He moved completely unaware of his size. As the creature approached his gaze became frightened as if a horrible truth fell upon him.

"You aren't the Whoez, are you?" he gasped.

"No. At least, I don't think so. What is the Whoez? Should I be looking for it?"

The creature shuddered and clenched at the name.

"They say the Whoez is a wandering spirit, a warrior scalped in battle. He is not the kind of folk you should be looking for. That's like looking for a healthy poison. It might exist, but if so, it couldn't be tasted without horrifying consequences. The Whoez is the roaming contradiction. Its existence is a battle of opposites, the Whoez would be the opposite of himself. He's dead, yet alive. He's maimed, yet still hunts. He's all he's supposed to be but in a rotten way; the best and the worst you'll ever see. He's beyond nature.

"Have you ever seen him?" I asked with intrigue.

"Oh, no! Only a few of us have ever seen the Whoez and lived. Because of him, my entire people are afraid to come out this way. He's a terrible thing."

"Sounds like a boogeyman."

"What's a boogeyman?"

"It's a pretend monster that people attribute to anything to make other people scared. You might not have anything to worry about." I said, hoping to reassure the on edge creature.

"No, no, no... The Whoez is real! Then, as if he'd forgotten that he was the one to bring up the Whoez, he stiffened with anger and accused me. "Why are you arguing with me? You are the Whoez aren't you?"

"Um, no... I never heard of him before I met you." I said trying to excuse myself. I could tell he was not satisfied with my answer so I tried changing the topic as quickly as I could. "What do you do?"

"Do? I don't do anything. Am I supposed to do something?" He responded insecurely. His posture dropped from his tense, defensive state, to a childlike soft and loose fidget. "I always figured doing things was a way to stay happy, but I'm already happy."

"I could tell. You were singing quite the happy song."

"I was singing again and you heard it? Oh, no no no... I must have sounded awful."

"No, you were really good." I assured him.

"Thank you. Thank you." He blushed modestly. "I used to sing all the time when I was younger. My sister and I would sing as loud as we could and rattle the walls. She was the best. She always knew how to keep me from making silly mistakes like getting too hungry. She'd say 'We are responsible for the condition of the world, so if you want it to be better, make it better.' We traveled all through this mountain, ate together, played, everything... until... she swallowed a Seedle."

"What's a Seedle?" I asked. Piop thought for a moment then sniffed the ground. When he came to a spot that caused him to stop he began using his large claws to dig until he found a slithering tail. He grabbed and pulled what appeared to be a giant centipede-like creature. The insect-like body was nearly 4 feet long and several inches thick, with many stubby little legs, all wiggling from segments leading up to a snake like diamond shaped face with insect-like pincers. It was horrifying. The creature tried biting and stinging Piop with a vicious hiss. However, Piop was unamused, squeezing the Seedle in his hands, turning the rigid body into sections of bloody mush.

"This is a Seedle." He said, presenting the twitching remains of the horrifying creature with outstretched arms. "She must not have chewed it enough because a while later she was complaining about a pain in her stomach. Before either of us realized it, the mandibles cut through her stomach. She cried a lot... bled a lot. I tried to help her. My sister's pain stretched infinitely until that final breath when she stopped moving. I had to bury her... Here in these caves... Alone. I'd never had someone that close to me die before, you know?"

"Yeah, I do know." I said reassuringly. "Losing innocence can be difficult, but returning to it is impossible."

I was stunned. The monster who only moments before sang without a care in the world, while I listened with all the pleasure I could siphon from the tune, found a way to be happy with little to no immediate consideration of his traumatic past. I envied his simple minded resolution. This creature said he doesn't do anything, but he probably doesn't realize just how much he's done, or will do.

Piop examined the Seedle and began eating the mush from his hands. Then with a trembling shutter in his throat, he swallowed hard.

"Are you okay?"

"Don't worry about me." Piop forced a smile. "I'm happy, remember. Besides, I'm not tired of this life yet..." I realized that you have two options when you get older, either learn to manage pain, or let it ruin you. When I'd get hurt my sister would say 'Pain is meant to stop us from danger, but sometimes we need to shut it off to go further. You have to get stronger because new problems come along every day.' I know there's more out there, beyond the grave, and a face to look into at the end of life to say "Thank you!"

I learned in that cave that the conviction of a monster is more valuable than the apathy of a man. Even wild things know love and loss.

★★★★★

I sat with Piop in silence as the creature lamented. Then, with a loud gurgle in his gut, his countenance shifted again and he wandered off through the cave. The light seemed to flee past him as though disturbed by his grumbling stomach noises, settling in small pockets. I wasn't sure if I should stay or go. I had no idea if the cave would be safer than the cliff or whatever was beyond it. After careful consideration, I left.

Chapter 5:
The Ashwoods

Leaving the cave was a strange experience. Unlike at home, when I'd gone from my dark basement to a bright day with painful clenching of the eyelids to adjust, the light seemed to act consistently between the two areas. I was now out in the open, once again staring over the edge of the cliff. The world had interesting landscapes including stretches of forests and lots of water. I examined the rock formations, planning my descent before climbing down the path, hand over foot.

I slid towards the edge into a sitting position, crawling on my hands and feet like a crab which seemed like a good idea at the time. The bird-dog came back, prowling and taking nips at my fingers. If not for my class ring making it hard to get a good bite I might have lost a finger. I tried avoiding him, but he kept at it. I would swat, he would dodge. He followed me all the way down the cliff to a large clearing, taking one last bite that pulled a small piece of skin off of my forearm. Once my feet hit the ground he tried running back up, but I jumped and grabbed him. I threw him down in anger and yelled.

"WHAT? YOU WANT TO EAT ME? HERE... HAVE MY FOOT!" I kicked the animal before he could recover from the football spike. His body went limp against the rock. Despite the aggravation, his pathetic state made me feel sorry for the thing. I don't know if it was the pity I felt or a deep seeded long-suffering desire for a pet I've had since I was a kid, but I took off my wide leather band watch, pulled the lace from the hood sewn into the jacket and fashioned a leash.

"Easy now... I'm not going to hurt you..." I tried assuring it. "Unless you bite me again. Then I'm going to barbeque you." The creature stood onto a shaky leg and hobbled.

I put the collar on the dazed creature, picked it up, and began walking. His body was tense at first, muscles flexed and claws dug in deep. I resisted the pinch and kept walking. After the first mile he relaxed the bird's muscles and by the second he held the appearance that he actually enjoyed the ride. Considering the brutal attack I gave him, he was probably thrilled I wasn't trying to hurt him anymore. At least for the moment, we made peace.

I walked aimlessly, trying to think of names for my new companion. I don't know why but I couldn't get Virgil out of my head. We had been reading Dante's Inferno in school and my teacher made a big deal about Virgil being Dante's guide through Hell. I didn't think I was in Heaven or Hell, but I was lost and this little animal knew more than I did, and his brokenness was something to pity; so Virgil it was.

I happened upon a wooded area which seemed to bow in such a way as to encourage an intricately specific entryway. A wall of trees began as if unable to extend beyond an invisible barrier in such a precise manner, I concluded it must have been a manmade wall. It seemed as though the signs of society I was looking for may lie within, so I pursued the path until I stood before a gaping hole carved into the woods.

The entrance was intimidating. An archway had been broken through, creating a sort of path, but the trees that were broken had been folded inwards, leaving large piles of logs and sticks that seemed to form a sort of bridge. The road carved in was exhaustible and difficult but absolutely direct. By then Virgil had perked up enough to cling, painfully, to my shoulder.

The Ashwoods were stunning. The air remained thick but settled into layers of fog. The living light glowed dully here, like wisps of dying embers. The ground below was covered in ash, which I assume you expected since it is a place called the Ashwoods, but the tree tops were round and lush with green. It seemed peculiar that the ash continued to fall from above the canopy of green, yet their color never dulled. It was as though the thick fog of ash was an intangible mist until after it lowered under the canopy of leaves. Somehow, in its descent, it became more physical in nature and lay to rest upon the forest floor. Through the thicket, I saw a strong amber glow concentrated afar off. Such forwardness had caused further apprehension. I continued climbing; branch over limb until the source of the light became apparent.

The path ended at what appeared to be an enormous tree, with a section hollowed out for a large oven, which burned intensely through the core. The heat was more manageable than the brightness of the fiery sun within. Atop the tree was a chimney of sorts, which allowed the smoke to pour out, leading directly into a break in the tree top canopy to the sky. I didn't know what to make of this new place, or where I should go next. The path had ended, and the stretch of the Ashwoods continued beyond my vision. So I took the moment to rest in the warm glow of the furnace.

I was nearly asleep when the sound of clanking metal had startled me. Coming up from the same path I entered the Ashwoods on, was a mighty man, clanking with metal tools, carrying large fruit. He was dark skinned, with unkempt straw-like hair, and his posture seemed adapted to the path. He was hunched a bit, with bow legs which managed to find the right steps with little to no notice. I contemplated running or hiding, but my actions and my thoughts had been removed from one another. Before I had known it, I yelled out...

"Hello? Who goes there?" The words started deep and imposing but cracked with doubt and regrettable phrasing. The man didn't seem to notice. Once he came closer, I noticed he was muttering to himself almost angrily. He kept his pace all the way to the burning tree chanting "All day, every day, every single hour. Never a break, always awake. Every minute soured." When he arrived, our eyes met and his age became far more apparent. He was dark skinned, strong, chiseled, but old, grey, and urgently fatigued.

I called out to him again. "Hello. Who are you?" The man's face brightened as if he all at once realized that I was there.

"Hello." he said back with gruff.

"Hi." I returned again. I couldn't think of much to say. "Are you the Whoez?"

The man glared deep at me. He was not amused. I wasn't sure if that meant he was the Whoez or hated the

Whoez or somehow both, but it was clear that the
question was not appreciated. I struggled to think of
anything that could inquire further without offending
the bruting soul. I resorted to child like thinking as I
asked, "What is your name?"

"My name? Oh, I'm Oo-Phoo." the man replied,
enchanted by the unexpected question. "You're not
from around here..."

"No sir." I confirmed.
"I can tell you know. Since... "He stopped mid
sentence, pointing up and down at my body as if to say
the obvious appearance was evidence enough. Then he
continued "It would take someone pretty lost to not
know who I am."

"Are you famous or something?" I asked.

The man erupted into a violent laugh. His body
jarred for a good minute before being interrupted by an
even more violent cough, followed by a sneeze. Once
he regained his composure, paused for a moment then
asked, "What did you say again?"

"Are you royalty or chief or something?" I tried repeating, partially embarrassed.

"No, no, no..." Oo-Phoo chuckled. "I make the clouds."

"That's a strange job. Do clouds need to be made? I thought they make themselves just fine."

"Clouds make themselves... HA! You are a strange little guy aren't you? Clouds can't make themselves. How would they know what shape to be, and when to pass the sky? You seem like a nice kid, and I have about 20 seconds to spare so I'll teach you what you need to know." the man said, inching closer, putting his lumbering arm over my shoulder.

"Here in the Furtherland, there was no way to discern time."

"Why don't you look at the sun, or just make a watch?" I stated matter of fact pointing to Virgil's collar. Oo-Phoo did not look amused.

"Sun?" he raised his brow unamused.

"Yeah, the big bright thing in the..." I looked up but couldn't see much of anything beyond the smoke and the trees. Thinking for a moment, I wasn't even sure I'd seen the sun or anything like it since I arrived. So rather than continuing, I clenched my teeth and lowered my head. He took this as a sign of admission that I actually knew less than I hoped, granting him satisfaction in being the authority on his own world.

"You see BOY," he stressed the 'boy' part of his sentence to further cement his authority; "the sky is a delicate thing. It can't think or do much of anything. But it has these pockets of currents that move. There is nothing in the pockets, so for a long time no one could see them or even knew they were there. That was until I put a cloud into the pocket. The cloud sits and travels all around the world until it comes back here where the cloud rests." He motioned towards the ash, indicating that the ash was somehow a tangible remain of the clouds ending their journey.

"I see..." I said, uncertain what this all meant. It hardly mattered because he continued lecturing.

"So every hour I bring fruit to this tree and throw it in. Moments later the cloud comes out. I make the cloud look like anything I want. My art is the most witnessed and yet unappreciated necessity in all of the Furtherland."

He took out a sharp knife from a sheath made from an animal pelt on his hip and began to shave the fruit into intricate sculpt of a wild bird. "Art is about meaning, but meaning doesn't come from art. Good art portrays meaning in the fastest most direct way it can... like my clouds. Anyone who looks up in the sky knows exactly what my clouds mean. No one else has a job like me. No one knows how hard it is."

"So why don't you take a break?"

Once again the man erupted into a full body laugh, complete with a cough, then sneeze, exactly like the first time. "I can't take a break. It takes me nearly an hour to gather the fruit and come back."

"Let an hour go without making a cloud." I said, hoping it would be some kind of revelation.

"I can't."

"Why not?" I insisted.

"I just can't. When you get older you'll realize that responsibility is more than only doing what you want to do, but more about doing it when you're supposed to." Then, while looking to the sky, as though he could see through the treetops he said. "It's time." He threw the large carved fruits into the tree, before turning to leave.

"Can I come with you?" I called.

"You can if you want, but you can't hold me up anymore." the man answered without so much as a backward glance then continued to repeat his song… "All day, every day, every single hour. Never a break, always awake. Every minute soured."

I considered following for a moment, but before I could decide he had already traced his way down the path and out of sight. I almost chased after him until I realized that I can always come back and find him here. Right now was not the time to be walking in circles. I needed to find someone that could help.

Chapter 6:

The Dense Emergent

I saw water off into the distance, past the dense emergent and decided to attempt to cool down from the sweat and heat that had been building up on my clothes over the hours of wandering. The grass was wet. Shallow water pooled at the surface pushing up lush herbs.

Large stumps jutted from the dirt at all angles high into the sky. There were no branches, not even a hint of them, and the thick roots weaved through the soil as if threaded intentionally. Lime green moss spiraled around the stumps linking each one to another. Small flowers grew in patches, with a strange mist around them. It wasn't until I happened upon a patch that I noticed the sweet smell.

The mist I could see rising from the flowers smelled strongly of ginger. Little bugs seemed to fly towards the mist as if drawn into it. When the bugs landed on the flower, it became apparent the flower was lined with pincers; which I had mistaken for thorns at first glance. The pincers grasped the bugs and excreted a gelatin which began dissolving them. The sound was horrific, immediate, and only loud enough to travel a few feet before dissipating altogether.

I let Virgil down and in no time, he found some crab-like creature, killed it, and began to eat. His beak was fully suited at puncturing and crushing portions of the shell, picking out the meat inside. I was tempted to take a taste of my own until I considered the possibility of the crab being filled with unknown parasites. I knew I'd need to focus and take more notes now than I ever had before, since this new place, the Furtherland, was filled with new dangers I'd never considered before.

A chipping noise echoed off the empty sky. With no particular path to go, I took up Virgil's leash and started following the noise, which seemed as good an idea as any.

The land built up higher before dipping suddenly. The grass and dirt diffused into white sand, against the milky sky, which reflected off unmoving glassy water. The display was so beautiful and yet so blank. Any number of colors could have filled the entire canvas of the site, but there was something so pleasing in seeing something that held the false appearance of emptiness.

I panned the water until I noticed a small shadowy human figure a ways off so I walked towards it. The figure was crouched with a flat, sharp-brimmed hat worn so low I could't see their face. I moved nonchalantly towards the person, hoping to seem as though I fit in enough to pass by, or hoping a conversation would find itself naturally through an exchange of pleasantries.

"Beautiful day..." I said. The figure looked up, allowing only one eye to peek out of the hat. It was a boy. The clothes were baggy and the stature not yet revealed, but the portion of the face I could make out seemed young, maybe 9 or 10 years old, with dark skin and light hair. I tried again. "What are you doing out here?" He maintained his silence. I took this as a sign to just keep moving.

I had gotten about 5 steps past the boy when he cleared his throat. I paused thinking it might be an invitation to continue speaking.

"Can you help me, sir?" I said more respectfully now, rather than the patronizing tone I must have had in my previous question.

"Sure. What do you need?" The boy responded. His voice held strong foreign accent with a faint resemblance to the Louisiana Bayou.

"My name's Dominick... this is Virgil." I said pointing to the scared bird-dog which climbed back up to my shoulder. "I've found myself in this place by accident and I have no idea where to go."

"You say you got here by accident. That must have been some accident. I've never accidentally been anywhere."

I scratched the back of my head, slightly embarrassed. "So who are you?"

"I'm Makya, the Huntsman."

"Ha. That's impossible. You're only a little boy." The words blurted out and were immediately regretted.

"You shouldn't try to correct somebody when you're so confused." he sneered.

He had me. He was completely right. I had no idea of anything and had no right to question the only person available to help. "I'm sorry."

"It's okay." he assured me. "Next time, hold your tongue long enough to keep yourself from sounding foolish. So where are you going?" he asked.

"I'm not sure." I replied. I hadn't thought about it much. I'd hardly been in the Furtherland, I wasn't sure if I wanted to go home yet, or even if getting home was possible.

"Well, knowing where you are going is the first step in determining the best way to get there, don't you think? Do you know what you're going to do while you're here?"

"Umm..." I thought for a moment. "Do you know who the Whoez is?"

"The Whoez... Yeah, I've heard that name before. You better be careful, I've heard some unsettling things about the Whoez."

The boy reached into a bag on his hip, pulling out a handful of grain with metal discs mixed in. The discs appeared to be razor sharp and with little caution he picked them out of grain in one hand with his index and thumb from the other, storing the picked ones in the palm of his second hand.

"So what is your business with the Whoez?" The boy's hazel eyes were locked on mine though his hands shuffled the discs and tossed them sideways into the pond as if skipping them. His undistracted actions were distracting and I found it hard to focus on a thought as my eyes darted between his face and his hands.

"Oh, no. I've never met the Whoez. When I first came here I met a stranger who warned me about the Whoez but was a bit vague and confusing about the details." I was careful to omit that Piop was a monster in a cave since I wasn't sure if calling him a monster would get my big mouth into more trouble. While I was talking, Makya emptied his bag of grain on to the sand and threw it into the ocean holding onto an attached string.

"Mm Hmm..." he said with firm evaluation.

"What are you doing?" I asked, interrupting my own train of thought.

"Goodness! You don't know anything, do you?" the boy chuckled, reeling in the bag by the long string. "I'm getting lunch."

"I'm sorry, I can't figure this place out. I'm glad you know what you're doing, but everything here seems to defy logic." I said in an attempt to excuse myself.

"I always thought logic is best defined by what works." Makya affirmed, then reached into the bag and pulled out one of several turtle like fish things with a disc-shaped hole clear through it. "Are you hungry?"

Chapter 7:
The Oval Town

Makya brought me to the first and only place in the Furtherland which resembled civilization. The first and only assembly of people, with the only buildings I'd see there. Shocking to me, the people weren't primitive, or tribal, or anything that I'd have expected given the rural nature of the Furtherland. They appeared to be united in social structure and fairly modern for not having electric commodities. Men and women walked around laughing and performing tasks reminiscent of old western movies.

Homes, built in a similar fashion, arranged nearly side by side in an oval formation, all facing outward. The bottom portion of the homes were built from giant solid curved stones. The roofs were gray slate stone, layered like scales which spiraled like steps off the back side and came to a point at the top. The doors and windows were a deep red wood. The only thing that differentiated the homes from another were strange symbols which were built into the roof by arranging white slate stone

At the bottom of the oval formation was a large windmill which faced what appeared to be a graveyard about a hundred yards away. The windmill was built in a similar fashion as the homes but had multiple layers of the large white stone stacked before coming to the slate stone peak. There was a ring of rusted metal blades which appeared to be working on rusted metal gears, which almost seemed out of place considering the ancient stone structure of the town.

The center of the oval was the social area. It seemed as though the people shared the well and the fire as communal property. The well had a 4 foot stone shell, yet it appeared to be steaming with near boiling water.

The fire pit had a 3 foot stone shell encircling it, but as I approached, I noticed that it was literally a pit. The hollow stone cylinder sank down far, funneling the escaping tongues of flames imprisoned within. It seemed altogether possible that a vein of molten magma ran side by side a vein of water within the terrain, both of which fed into the heart of the town.

All the intricacies were nearly familiar, yet held such a peculiar alteration as if to constantly remind me I'd lost the reality I'd known. There were metal poles about 6-feet-long evenly spaced through the town, behind the houses in a circle. Atop the poles were beautiful 8 sided diamonds of varied colors, or as my geometry teacher would say 'it formed completely equilateral octahedron". The diamonds glowed with a uniform pulse which slowly intensified and dimmed, faintly resembling street lamps. It was comforting seeing something so relatable, even if I really had no idea why they'd need lights in a place which appeared to always be lit. I walked through, looking around in awe for a moment before feeling more out of place among the people than I had in the wild.

I was occasionally self-conscious, particularly with the scars on my cheek and hairline. I knew there were things about me I'd change if I could. I was 5'10''', 175 pounds with a somewhat muscular build. I'd played football for a few years as a receiver, so I could run and take a hit. I wasn't entirely popular, but with Tony as my brother, I was known enough. Still, I had the luxury of being able to blend in with the crowd. However, I had no chance of blending in here. I looked different from them. While they ranged in age, height, and overall shape, as would any group of people, their features all seemed to be molded from a uniform source. Their skin was dark, almost reddish, and they all grew thick straw yellow hair. I was olive skinned and my hair was much darker, nearly black, with short curly locks. All their smoldering hazel eyes met my two cobalt blues.

No two people wore identical anything. It was clear their attire was all hand made, and clearly done with great skill and intricate craftsmanship. The style appeared vaguely reminiscent of something Asian, almost Indian, and was unusually refined, multi-layered dress, that somehow maintained a touch of casual looseness to accommodate their physical lifestyles.

The difference didn't appear to work in my favor at the moment. I felt out of place and on trial. The entire village was looking at me.

I knew that look all too well… it was the same kind of look the student body would give when a new kid transferred in the middle of the year. They were the outsider, being evaluated. Girls would whisper, guys would glance and either nod their heads in greeting or turn away without concern. I'd never been the new kid until now. It was interesting. Even in the Furtherland, the people continued these practices, but given the stone homes and open atmosphere, these common high school gestures seemed primal. In some ways it showed we haven't progressed as far in the first world as we'd like to think. Everything qualifies for public judgment. Though, it also testified more to the universal relatability that binds all cultures. People are people in every place and time.

On the way, Makya told me they were the Amank people. I kept thinking of them as tribal, but they were far more civilized than their humble environment lead on. Much like at home, the people were in constant motion, seeming to know exactly where they needed to be and what needed to be done. The only difference was their pace was much slower. They didn't seem to worry about haste. The day was endless... They lived within shouting distance of anyone they could ever know. Their actions were so close to familiar but strangely missing the chaos that I'd grown accustomed to. There were children though none of them cried. There were men working, but none of them shouted in anger. It was the exact kind of precision one might expect to find if you were to examine an ant colony... a system of individuals working towards a common goal for the whole.

Such a thing rarely worked in my world. I'd seen people come together in the wake of a tragedy, setting their egos aside just long enough to restore a portion of what was lost. Yet, before long, they'd all retreat to their own lives. I was no exception. I'm still not. Perhaps that was the major difference between our peoples; one lived by the burden of others, the other lived by the burden of pride.

An older woman took a step into my path, staring through me with disgust. "Are you tamed or untamed?" she probed.

"I'm not sure. Is there a difference?" I responded, feeling a bit nervous about the attention I was getting.

"Untamed things are destructive nuisances. They hurt on impulse." the woman said coldly as if reprimanding a child.

"I suppose I'm tame then." I responded with an uncertain smile.

The woman smiled back. "Good! We can't have any untamed creatures here. They must be killed."

"If you kill what is untamed, wouldn't that make you untamed?" I pointed out the hypocrisy.

"Of course not. Tamed creatures have the courtesy of making a policy of the harm they do."

I didn't know how to respond, so I nodded and continued walking. Some men stood with tools in hand, welcoming me with a respectful nod. I couldn't help but feel the distinct burn of some girls staring a hole through me. I tried to keep my eyes forward.

I followed Makya to a house with a symbol on the roof similar to the disc used to catch our lunch. The disc appeared to be a symbol for these people in the same way an arrow would indicate a hunter to many of the tribes of my world. This house was where Makya lived. Inside were two women, a man, and a toddler.

The man appeared to be quite strong at first glance. It seemed obvious that he must be Makya's mentor and possibly his father. This fact seemed all the more apparent when I noticed a portion of his leg was missing. His calf was entirely mangled, disfigured to the bone, as though he'd had a bite taken out of him.

"Hello sir."

"Come in. Call me Nock." the man motioned kindly for me to come in.

"Thank you, Nock." I said with an unintentional bow. Something about the new culture and the familiar Asian attire made me feel that a bowing gesture would be received as respect. He didn't seem to care either way. "I'm Dominick and this is Virgil. I hope you don't mind him in your house."

"You named your food?"

"I hadn't decided if I was going to eat him when I named him, but I guess he's my pet now. Is having a pet a strange thing here?"

"Animals in the house are usually food. But I have to say I'm impressed. I've never seen anyone catch one of these Joco-birds. Kill them sure... but never catch one. You must be pretty quick."

"Heh, I guess." I said in embarrassed modesty. "So, Makya is your boy?"

"He sure is." the man said, beaming with pride.

"Did you teach him to hunt and catch fish? He was skillfully impressive. More impressive than any skill I've known, especially for such a young boy." I said affirming his pride.

"Let me tell you something... Men are limited of power in our youth because we don't have the discipline to use it. My son has the discipline most people never develop, granting him skills most people never obtain." Nock said with a reserved smile, as though admitting to himself that his son has become what he could no longer be and others would never achieve. "So where will you go from here?"

"I don't know. Is there somewhere I should go?"

"Depends on where you came from. I'm sure you could stay in town with us for a while while you figure it out."

"Thank you for your hospitality. I'm actually from another world."

"Aren't we all." He chuckled.

"Wait? Are we?" I questioned. Nock shrugged. "Is there at least a prophecy or anything that people say that can be helpful?" I asked hopefully, still trapped in the ancient culture mindset.

"HA! A prophecy! That's ridiculous. People here don't know the past and they hardly know the present, you can't expect them to know the future. You'd have a better chance of making up a prophecy than finding one here."

"What is the past to you?" I pressed. "You all seem human, and I'm shocked that we seem to be speaking the same language."

"Of course we're human." Nock said with humorous offense.

"Then how did you get here?"

"I imagine the same way as you did."

"...And how is that?"

"You know it's funny, I can't really remember. It's been such a long time and the past becomes cloudier with each passing cloud."

"Wonderful." I sighed.

"Hold on... MAKYA!" Nock called out abruptly. "Go get the letter jar in my room."

"Yes, Father." The boy said with reverence.

"I wrote a letter once, when we first came here, in case someone found our little town past our time. I meant for it to be a chronicle of our people and never finished it. It was written long ago, so I don't exactly remember what's in it. Probably not much, but it might have some answers.

"Here you go." the boy handed the jar to me. Inside was a curled up scroll with yellowed fabric. The edges were wrinkled but appeared wholly intact.

"Thank you so much. If you don't mind, I'll read it later."

"There's no rush."

"I see." Suddenly the conversation fell into awkward silence. I didn't know if I should stay or leave. With the letter in hand, it seemed impolite to press for more answers and I didn't want to read it while he was sitting in front of me. I thought long and muscled up a single inquiry "What do you think I should do?"

"I'm sorry but I'm not much of a thinker, but since you're here try to enjoy it."

I stayed in Nock's home for the day, resting. It occurred to me that I hadn't had a moment to sit since I went running what felt like days ago. While I recovered, Makya picked vegetables in the community garden and his sisters prepared the turtle-fish he killed. I felt like I should help, but Nock insisted I stay with him, answering questions he had about our world, laughing wildly at modern customs he found absurd. He couldn't believe we wash our waste away with clean water. No matter how I tried to justify Western American culture in the 21st century, he felt entitled to mock without reservation. At least he believed me.

★★★★★

Hours passed. We all ate together, mostly in silence, as the family watched me. Makya chewed thoroughly on every bite, while Nocks daughters Vaesti and Aeya, shot various implying glances. We traded pleasantries and then swapped stories, all the while I built up the courage to ask about the Whoez.

"Do you mind if I ask about the Whoez?" I inquired with reluctance.

"The Whoez... Psh. That's your boy, Tuk-Rah, isn't it Vaesti." Nock mocked towards Aeya, the older of the two sisters. I couldn't help but grin as I watched Aeya hold back her smile.

"It's not Tuk-Rah. He wouldn't be doing those things..." Vaesti barked.

"What things?" I interrupted.

"The boy lost his head, started dressing like an egg, and went on a killing spree."

"It wasn't him!" Vaesti continued in protest. "And if it was, he didn't kill any Amank... only those mountain devils."

"Then why didn't he come back?" Nock shouted, silencing the group.

The older sister sat with her hands in her lap in silence. I didn't know if I should press the matter or let it die. Nock, who already had the final word, felt it necessary to add for clarity where he stood on the issue.

"We have rules. We only kill what we eat or to protect. We don't go murdering animals out of some sick campaign, especially when the Stonecoats feed the light. Am I clear?"

"Yes father..." the four submitted. It was interesting how things here felt so much like home.

"What is the light? Is it alive" I asked, breaking the tension of the group.

"We're not sure how exactly, but it most certainly is alive. We call it the Sabanora. It encompasses the Furtherland with brilliant radiance, but as you've seen it likes to move in swarms."

"Yeah, it's pretty cool. It reminds me of lightning bugs or something..."

They all stared at me blankly for a moment. We continued to eat. The food was different, though not altogether exotic. The turtle-fish, was unlike anything I'd seen at home, but I'd hardly seen every fish in my world, so it was possible this was something our worlds shared. The fish tasted a bit like tuna but was more orange than dark purple. The pallet of my hosts seemed to prefer tart and spicy to my preferences of sweet and savory, but they didn't ruin the food by adding some disgusting ingredient or flavor.

The wine they served was nearly black and incredibly strong. I've had alcohol before, mostly at home, but never in the casual excess they drank it. Even Makya drank heavily. I dipped the bread they gave me into the wine, something I'd seen my dad do numerous times. They all choked down a laugh, then I laughed with them until I found myself sighing. I'm not sure how it snuck up on me, but all of a sudden I missed my family.

Nock's letter: The Furtherland

We were the Amank people. Protectors of the land. Keepers of the Spirits. Guides to the travelers. These travelers, the white men, arrived from various lands. The mingling of voices and confusion of speech taught us to adopt a uniform tongue, of which English seemed to be an intermixing of many of their languages, so in time that is what we all spoke. The Amank society was sustained and fertile, yet with the white men bringing new languages, arts, and tools we gladly exchanged information for protection.

Many tribes had vicious battles against one another and against the travelers, who being fewer in number, needed refuge while establishing themselves. They accepted our terms of natural balance, so we took them into our society and our relationship became interwoven. Together, it was declared that a new age was upon us. The dawn of the 18th Century. The travelers taught us their ways. We adopted their industry and masonry and together we built a strong civilization. Many battles were fought side by side against red and white men alike to protect the small kingdom we'd built. We were successful for many years, birthing new generations together, settling in the most unconventional manner. The assimilation of races between the European and Native people birthed a uniform red skin yellow-haired people; truly a new creation. I was one of such seeds in the blended generation, mixed between red and white, as was my wife, Kreeli.

Kreeli and I were young when we too became travelers. I was one of several hunters who stayed vigilant at night to protect our keep. One cloudless night the stars had vanished from the sky. We called out to our people, who aroused with marvel at the curious sight, clinging to one another in awe. We congregated together and stared up in wonder. The trees went still, the animals howled, and then the spirit of light descended upon us as falling stars, sweeping us up in a violent wind, pulling apart our world and bringing us to another.

This new world was bright, nearly eliminating all shadows, except for the passing intense glow from the cloud of swimming stars. There was no sun, no moon, and the spirits of the sky we knew had vanished. The milky sky had robbed us of measurement and without distinction between day and night, time had been lost. We knew nothing of this place, nothing of where, or when. Some of us speculated that we had all died by the falling stars and this world was the next, but our ancestors had not met us there. The loss of time became too much for some, as members of the tribe dispersed from the group in search for ways of recording time.

It was then that the Amank people fully understood the travelers' trial of reestablishment. Generations of world observation mean little when the entire world changes. To the Amank, knowledge of the land was crucial for survival. What was poisonous, what was edible, how long food cycles were, what animals were predators, which animals were prey... Everything we'd taught and passed down, countless generations of precious knowledge, gone in a moment. Those of us who could hunt, still hunted, but the meat in this world was less palatable. Many of us took turns sampling the vegetation to determine what could be eaten. We lost many loved ones in this way. In time, a pattern developed and our observations became successful and those of us who remained began to do well until additional problems began to arise. Without the calming darkness of night, our people became sick from an inability to sleep in the sustained luminescent air. Through fermentation, we were able to create a strong wine which aided in sleep which we took with each meal. In time, our bodies became adapted to the drink and we kept increasing our intake. For some of us, the drink isn't enough and small amounts of poisonous berries are taken to ensure deep rest.

In time we learned we weren't the only residents of the Furtherland...

Chapter 8:
The Windmill

The entire town appeared to have fallen asleep; all except me. Even Virgil found a perch next to me to curl up on for a catnap. Night never came in the Furtherland. There was no sun, no moon, and no stars. The sky slowly shifted in colors of pink to purple to pale blue, with clouds floating in lines as the town's marker for time. It's strange that here, people had to look up to learn time when I was so used to people looking down to find it on their watch or their phone.

I still didn't know how to read the cloud time and was marveled by the reality shift. I was at least able to determine that there were about 70 minutes between clouds, at least according to the glances I was able to make at the watch still wrapped around Virgil. I didn't know if the clouds were supposed to be 70 minutes apart or if Oo-Phoo had unintentionally slowed down the hours.

I decided to take the quiet opportunity to read Nock's note. The note was remarkable in content. These were not people from a lost world, rather a lost time not so long ago. He said the 18th century... I couldn't help but gawk at the paper as I read the strange circumstances that befell such a group, nearly the same circumstances that occurred to me. They were stuck here and all at once it occurred to me that the return back home may be impossible. A sudden unnerving chill made me jump to my feet. Sitting still for too long had given me time to realize I might be in a lot of trouble. I needed to take my mind off the weight of the situation. I dusted off my bottom and decided to roam the quiet town, finally taking the time to admire all the little details.

I knew no direction in the Furtherland, but if I were to stand in the center of the town, choosing the windmill at the top of the oval as my northern point, then the western area would have been designated to agriculture, whereas the eastern area looked to be designated for what passed as industry. The south was nothing more than a cobblestone path leading into the open world just enough to be found by mistake; almost as if they'd planned on having an unknown visitor. The thought of an alien was unsettling, even though that's what I was in many ways. They weren't afraid though. The town had no walls, no fences, not even a gate. The town lay on flat land with only meticulously placed cobblestones lining a large perimeter.

"Hello." Spoke a hoarse, yet femininely tender voice. I turned to see Aeya, the older of the two sisters who lived in Makya's house. Though we ate together, we hadn't interacted much. She was tall, broad, and exceptionally pretty. She had the lengthy figure similar to the girl soccer players at school. Her dark skin was sleek and shiny, and her sandy hair fell past her shoulders in an unkempt but completely sexy mess. Her hazel eyes met mine and I could see they were bright, nearly golden. I turned my head away in flirted shame.

"Hi..." I mumbled.

"How did you get here?" she asked.

"I have no idea. I was hoping one of you could tell me."

"Would you be mad if I brought you here?" she inquired nervously.

"Did you?" I perked up with intrigue.

"I don't know... maybe. I think I dreamed of you once... Of a white man."

"That's sweet." I said dismissively, frustrated at the false hope of her question. She followed my wandered steps until we came to the well where we both sat. "This place is so strange. I can hardly figure anything out. It's similar in so many ways, but then there are things that don't make sense... like the clouds, and monsters."

"Monsters? You saw a monster? What did it look like?" she asked excitedly.

"It was a large bruiting thing with thin arms and legs and covered in quills. He sang well, but seemed sad."

"Where was it?" her tone dropped, becoming solemn.

"It was in a cave on the cliffs out by the Ashwoods. But don't worry, he seemed like a nice monster."

Her face had hardened and her posture stiffened. "Do you remember an older woman when you arrived in town? She asked if you were 'tame or untamed?'"

"Yeah, I remember."

"That was Stikini. She asked if you were tame to see if you were like one of them, the Stonecoats, mountain devils. The Stonecoats used to be a thriving society of smiths who lived in a quartz city near our town. They built many wonders and even gifted our town with the blades to the mill as a peace offering. Then, they became feral beasts; tearing down their own civilization from the inside out and creating a chasm between our people."

"If they built a society, they couldn't be that bad.

Maybe they'll build it again."

"You don't understand... They aren't what they were. My father, Nock, was the huntsman before Makya. Alone, he would provide enough food for the entire town and by his sword was able to transform a group undertaking into a single manhunt. Close to perfect, he was careful and precise with his technique. I used to watch him for hours as he'd slay animals 3 times his size in fantastic battles to protect our town. He was never one to underestimate an opponent and treated each kill with fear and respect. No creature was more feared or respected by the huntsman than the Stonecoats.

It was mutual fear that kept our peoples safe. We couldn't use them for much. Their meat was horrendous, their pelts itchy and full of thorny quills. There wasn't ever a practical reason to kill the Stonecoats, except when they became unstable monsters. However, they moved far away into a pack of wandering beasts. Intermittently, one or two would incidentally find their way back towards our town.

Whatever changed them caused a drift between two

parts of the creature. Most of the time, the Stonecoats were peaceful and gentle, who would sing celestial songs that would feed the Sabanora. Sadly, the other part caused the Stonecoats to be incapable of controlling their appetites which grew larger and larger until the blood-lust erupted into a frenzy. Their viciousness knew no bounds and they'd consume anything they could find meat in, bloating their bellies in their gluttonous fits. The Sabanora, which thrived in the ethereal songs of the Stonecoats, became ill and corrupt by the vicious gnashing and howling. For this reason, the light would scatter once the Stonecoats reached its maximum craving.

The Amank people feared the Stonecoats' hunger, which came and went without regulation. The only warning was the fleeing light, which on a few occasions came too late for some of the Amank people. One such person was my mother who had been out with Makya for the day, teaching him to fish with the discs, much like she had done with all of us.

The sky became dark and filled with howling. My father grabbed his sword and ran towards the water and found the creature there, my mother dead in its mouth.

Without hesitation, my father killed the Stonecoats by chopping its head from its shoulders. In unmatched sorrow, my father began pulling what pieces of my mother he could find out of the beast's stomach to give her a proper burial. Makya saw the entire event, watching in horror as our father dripped with the mixture of blood and meat from our mother and her murderer. However, as my father stooped to grab her remains the severed head of the creature bit his leg, taking a large chunk out. The monster was dead, but the spirit of gluttonous hunger attempted to take its one last bite. My father crawled home that night... He was a stronger man then. It took a long time for my dad to let go of his own death wish, and now, he holds a contemptuous view of everyone... Everyone but Makya… and you. That horrible night, Makya walked back and forth between the water and town and gathered as much of our mother as he could hold. He made countless trips and by morning, our mother's body was whole and ready to be buried.

I can't say I blame them, the Stonecoats. Those monsters can't control themselves. Their hunger is so vicious they'd eat their own mother if they could, and probably had. When they become hungry, they are unstoppable demons." Aeya spoke with conviction and was clearly disturbed, possibly afraid, at the mention of Piop. She placed her hands between her legs and slouched, thinking intensely.

"I'm sorry..." I choked out. I had nothing of value to say other than offer my past due condolences.

"Can you stay with me?" she asked holding back tears.

"You don't need to worry. I'm sure they'll all wake up soon." I told her.

Looking back, I can hear how uncaring my words were, spoken with false assurance immersed in distracted thought. I should have paid more attention to what I was told, but perhaps more importantly, I should have paid attention to the words I said back.

Aeya sat with me for a while. At one point she even placed her head on my shoulders. I smiled at her once or twice, but my mind couldn't be further. I kept staring at the windmill.

"What's in the windmill?" I asked.

"Not much. Some tools, grain, that sort of things. We can go look if you want?"

"If it's okay, I'd prefer to be alone for a while."

★★★★★

I went to the windmill alone. It was a tranquil place so close to the town that no one seemed to mind my wandering there unescorted. The inside was unpredictably beautiful. The main floor was a polished emerald slate that seemed to tint the room with its green glow. There were racks of tools, built neatly into the stone walls, each encrusted with sparkling gems. The stairs were thick clear glass that adopted paler green from the glowing emerald floor. The steps dipped in the corner to a slightly lower landing, then spiraled along the wall to the top level.

The top level seemed much different. The floor was made of the same redwood the doors and windows of the town were made with, and the internal slate stone roof exposed gave an almost subterranean feel. The only sense of being elevated came from a sizable oval window which overlooked the town and allowed fresh air to whistle into the mill. The opposite end was where the internal mechanism of gears and cogs from the mill's blades, mated in a squeaking rotation. I was walking up to the window when I saw movement on the floor from the corner of the empty room. It startled me a moment with thoughts of wild animals who possibly nested there, but the movement had stopped. I went towards the window again and again I saw movement, this time in a more precise location. That is when I noticed the unframed mirror.

The same mirror which had been missing from the empty frame in my attic. It rested against the stone, reflecting the surrounding stone appearing nearly invisible. "How did this get here?" I wondered. I looked into the mirror for a while, hoping it would be some kind of magical gateway between worlds and allow me to pass through it as I did through the threshold to enter this world.

Nothing happened. I was disappointed. I looked out the window for a few minutes, enjoying the clean air breeze. Then, without meaning to, I fell asleep.

Aeya's Letter: The Chase

I *dreamed of a boy, a wonderful dark haired boy, whose skin matched the sand and who ran with wild intent. Though I see him in my sleep, rushing through as a translucent specter, I want him for my own. Not even in my slumber could I endure the fantastic chase to catch him. He was fast, sprinting with the wind at his back, nearly flying with long strides. Even the creatures failed to keep pace. In all that chases him, he escapes. Yet, while he eludes me, he always comes back... a re-occurring phantom sewn to my slumber.*

He finally came to me in the flesh, out of the blurred apparition of a far off dream, but doesn't remember the chase. I need to know. I need to discover what he is running towards as he runs away from me...

-Aeya

Chapter 9:
The Ruby Stairs

I awoke in water, drifting between two narrow shores at the bottom of a canyon. I had no idea how I'd gotten there and despite all the things I'd eventually learn about the Furtherland, I only have my suspicions about what actually happened. It seemed as though only a moment before I'd fallen asleep atop the windmill tower, and yet, I found myself pushed and pulled by an unrelenting tide, striking one coast, then another as the canyon pool churned.

When I gained my bearings, I clawed my way onto a sandy shore. A minute or two passed allowing me to catch my breath before noticing my surrounding environment consisted of high cliffs encircling the waking pond.

For a moment, it seemed as though I was stuck. I looked around for any pattern of rock I'd be able to climb, that's when I caught sight of stairs.

The stairs were detached ruby platforms set apart in fixed increments, scaling up the canyon walls, high above the cliffs, extending beyond the terrain and continued into the air. At first glance, it seemed to be a sure thing. I stepped onto the first platform, expecting it to dip under my weight, but the ruby was stiff and held in place without so much as a rattle. The higher I climbed the more platforms became apparent, as though they were camouflaged by the supporting sky. There was no hand rail, or wall to prevent falling. Each step was easy enough to take, however, the severe reality of a dangerous climb caused me to proceed with great care. To ascend was a final commitment, as any failed attempt would surely result in a fateful drop.

The cliffs top was close, extremely close, but the steps veered away from the land and hovered high above the bottom. There was no safe way to exit the ruby stairs. I contemplated going back down. I even took a step before realizing how awkward and dangerous climbing down actually felt. Going up seemed to be the better option.

The higher I climbed the more concerned I became. My strength was failing with no end in sight. I kept assuring myself that the stairs lead somewhere, but I had no idea if it was a place I should go. I stopped for a while to catch my breath. I had to be nearly 100 stories high with nothing but sky around me. The break satisfied the aches in my legs and allowed me to catch my breath.

I climbed further; the stairs now arranged in a spiral finally had an end up ahead. To that point, each stair led to another.... but the last stair. The last stair had nothing beyond it. I felt cheated, as though the challenge earned me a right to a new path. I spit off the side in anger, secretly hoping my action would become noticed by some mystical force. Nothing...

Climbing back down was tricky. My legs were already shaky from the climb up, but now I struggled to hold my balance and maintain an appropriate speed. My impatience caught me and a hurried misstep caused me to fall brutally down several of the jagged steps. I was bruised and cut but had managed to catch myself in the gaps before tumbling down into the water below. My leg hung over the side with such weight that I'm convinced something was trying to pull me down.

Blood dripped down various steps from the scrapes I'd gotten from falling. I can't say if that was the trick or not but the stairs began to pull apart and rearrange. I was incredibly terrified as I clung on to the platform I'd fallen on. It took some time to settle, giving me another well-needed rest before completing the descent. When I came close enough to the bottom, I saw where the stairs had actually found the ground at the top of the cliff and there, standing there waiting for me, was a masked person...

I knew I had found the Whoez.

His face was covered in some sort of mask, with an intricate ivory faceplate which resembled an egg shell fractured along what would be human features. The eyes were small, hollow, and haunting. The mask was merely the centerpiece of what appeared to be a large mane made of thick fur and lustrous feathers. He stood with a demanding presence which made him appear much taller than he was.

His breath rasped with a scratchy growl, like a wolf who won a fight from surviving their throat being ripped out. When my feet found solid ground the Whoez and I stood only feet apart, sizing one another up and finding our heights to be matched.

The Whoez was covered in an exotic French styled gentleman's habit à la française: the overcoat appeared to be dark blue with a high collar and thick, intricate gold embroidery trim. The waistcoat matched the style and color of the overcoat, though had only a slight depth of embroidered trim. White breeches matched in uniform tucked into long black stockings with pointy black boots.

Not a portion of skin was visible beneath the undoubtedly ill breathed, heavy clothing. He was horrifyingly still... the hollow eyes notched in the cracks of the mask were perfectly fixed in on me.

I knew I had no strength to fight after such a taxing climb and fall. I slouched a little, trying to catch my breath without doubling over. I noticed a sheathed rapier sword hanging from his hip, which he rested one white-gloved hand on. If the Whoez wanted me dead, here was his chance.

"I'm here." I said, trying to sound in frustration. "I found you. I won the game. Take me home." Somehow the words spilled out without thought behind them. I hadn't resolved to go home, but there it was. My only perceived chance now that I found the mystical folk menace of the Stonecoats and the Amank people.

"You're here now. You don't get to be anywhere else." The voice rasped.

"Did you do this to me? Did you drop me in this nonsense world with nothing? And for what? What could you want?" I took a swing at the Whoez in anger, missing wildly.

The Whoez lowered his head, dodging my ill executed attack then back up again. By the time the ivory face squared with mine, the Whoez had kicked me in the throat. I fell down hard, grabbing at my neck in an attempt to find breath and ease the pain. This was it, I thought staring up at the renown folk murderer, I might as well go out with a fight. I clawed my way to my feet and punched the Whoez in the face. The punch landed and caused him to stumble for a moment before he kicked me again, this time in the stomach. I went down again. Then with several nudges of the tall, long-toed boots I found myself at the edge of the cliff. I tried coming up with a plan to turn the situation around. I basically flailed about, trying to grab what I could.

I grabbed the Whoez's pants and yanked, hoping they'd come down to give me any bit of advantage to gain the upper hand. Instead, the Whoez punched me in the face, knocking me clear to the ground....

Then, he stomped my head.

Light faded into blackness, I was falling and then everything shattered.

Chapter 10:

Like Her

—•——//—ε✿ȝ—//——•—

Images faded in and out of shadows, as though a cloud passing over the moon and then, without so much as a detectable passing, the veil had gone like wind from where I was and the threshold which I had somehow passed through into the Furtherland had brought me back to the world I'd first known; the world only a day or so before I'd insist was the "real world".

It's hard to discern what reality is when experiencing multiple realities. They are both real, so it no longer becomes comfortable stating one is more real than the other. As the physical world can't exist without the metaphysical, so this reality is tethered to that of the Furtherland. Only then man realizes the substance which he is created by is intangible, opening reality to impossible discoveries.

I almost felt crazy, especially when I realized that I was outside near a park a few blocks away from my house, at night... I hated this park. I hadn't been afraid of the dark in years, but the sudden realization of standing somewhere without knowing how I arrived there frightened me. Despite the pain from falling down stairs and the concussed pain in my head from losing a fight, I somehow managed to run home.

My house was empty when I arrived, which was fine with me since I hadn't come up with a reasonable excuse for my parents on where I'd been. All I knew was that modern comforts are rarely appreciated enough. After a warm shower, a couple of hot pockets, and a wonderfully soft bed, I slept better than I ever had before. When I awakened, the events of the Furtherland had all faded into the realm of absurdity. The only rational conclusion was that it must have all been a dream.

Is there anything so open to infinite possibility as one's own dreams?

I could hear my parents arguing. My mother was shrill and my father was doing all he could to calm her down. I had no idea what was going on. I'd never heard them quarrel so seriously, even after what had happened. I tried keeping my breath quiet enough to make out what they were saying.

The longer I listened, the more I realized that my parents were arguing about me. I didn't know for sure how long I'd been gone if time passed the same in the Furtherland as it did here, but it was apparent that I was gone long enough for my parents to become completely infuriated. They had seen that I came home and couldn't decide how to handle me.

My mother kept shrieking "This is all my fault." While my dad assured her with a stern tone. "It's not your fault. He can't be doing this."

My dad begged my mother to calm down. I couldn't tell how long the conversation had gone on, but by this point, my dad was fuming. He pounded on the wall with his fist. "He can't treat us like this. He has to be punished."

I didn't know if I should get out of bed and confront him in an attempt to calm him down or if I should just pretend to be asleep until he calmed on his own.

Suddenly I remembered the time when I'd taken my dad's car for a joyride. I had my license for a month or so and took the car without asking. I returned each aspect to its default position; I parked in the exact same spot, turned the radio back to his last station, adjusted the mirrors, and then adjusted the seat... Apparently the order I did this in left the mirrors far more askew than I meant to and my dad, after asking my mom and brother, Tony, if they'd taken his car, knew it was me. They thought I was planning to run away or something.

I remember I was pretending to sleep when he stormed in my door and shouted at me, "What the Hell do you think you're doing taking my car out? Do you want to make your mother worse?"

"I don't care." I snapped back in defense. I couldn't believe that I'd actually told him I didn't care. He slapped me in the face hard, knocking me down. It was the first time in years he'd used any physical discipline and the shock of it rattled me. I stormed out of the house. I wasn't going to run away but the more I thought of it, it did sound more and more like a good idea.

That was over a year ago, and things hadn't been the same between us. Neither of us apologized for our actions. There wasn't even a mention of it in the house. And truthfully I didn't blame him; I blamed my mother. I got out of bed quietly, put on my jeans, and opened the door. They both froze. The argument stopped. Their countenances shifted. My mother ran away from me weeping while my dad stood back, arms folded as though he was choosing his words carefully.

Suddenly, my mother ran back and threw herself at me. She hugged me hard, then kissed me, crying hysterically and kept saying "I'm sorry, I'm sorry" over and over. She hadn't hugged me in years and I wasn't sure if I was comfortable with her doing so. It didn't matter, however, since shortly thereafter she began yelling at me. "Where were you? Why did you leave?

ARE YOU ON DRUGS? I"VE BEEN AWAKE FOR THREE WHOLE WEEKS! ARE YOU TRYING TO KILL ME!?!?!?!" She was not happy. I could hardly process what was happening.

"No, I was…" I had no answer. "Let's sit down and talk and I'll try to tell you what happened." I didn't want to talk to her, but I couldn't even process what I experienced or what I should be saying. I figured if I could buy time and create a situation to discuss on my own terms things would go better.

"TELL ME NOW DOMINICK! WHERE WERE YOU?!" She demanded.

"I DON'T HAVE TO TELL YOU ANYTHING!" I shouted back. Motioning like I was about to run out of the house.

"Please, Dominick! Don't go. I just… let's just sit down and have some coffee." she begged.

The power in the conversation shifted. My mother and I had a disturbed past and we both knew that no matter how right she was in any given situation all I'd need to do was swing the weight of guilt. Still, my dad was harder to manipulate. I needed time to come up with a story. I couldn't tell the truth, right? Maybe I could say I was at Cody's, my best friend's house…

only, that was probably the first place they looked. I needed to think of something.

My mom was quiet just long enough to put a pot of coffee on. She shook with rage and anxiety through the entire process, spilling small amounts of water and grounds. She went to the cabinet and took her pills with a tall glass of water then with impatience baiting on her breath she said "I'm ready."

My story, still not fully developed, I began with a question. "Do you know what a vision quest is? It's where a Native American boy goes into the wild to find himself by connecting with nature." I said, gauging her response.

"You're not Native American, Dominick. You're ITALIAN!!!" my mom replied with frustration. She was not amused, but I continued since it was the closest thing to the truth that didn't sound absolutely crazy.

"I had a last minute, once in a lifetime chance to experience the exact same thing. I was alone, left to my strength and wits. The nights were cold, but I had to push through... I had to..."

"What kind of BS story are you trying to feed us? Do I look stupid, Dom?" My dad said sternly.

"It's about a girl, isn't it?" Tony said coming into the room. I was shocked he was at home. Last I'd seen him he was off at college.

"No... it was... um..." I said in offense before contemplating what else it could have been.

My dad's face softened a bit.

Then, with a relieved chuckle, Tony teased, "I knew it. He was with a girl."

"You skipped three weeks of school for a girl?! They might hold you back an entire year now!" My mother exploded, quickly returning to her coffee to keep herself quiet.

"I... No! I was on a vision quest!" I said, unable to buy my own story.

"...with a girl...?" My dad insisted. The words resembled the taunting of my brother Tony.

"That's not like you Dominick. I'd expect that from your brother, but not you." My mother said with disgust.

"You expect that from me?" Tony fabricated offense.

"Shut up, Tony!" My dad cut in. "You can't do that Dom…" Next time you decide to run out with some girl, use some common sense and bring your cell phone. You can't just disappear and act like everything's okay. You need to come home, every night, and if you're out late, you need to call and let us know where you're going to be."

I didn't know what to say. They were extremely upset but somehow relieved that I was alive and not on drugs that they could tell. They were completely content to believe I'd shacked up with some girl for a few weeks. I couldn't help but feel a little happy that my dad thought I had it in me to do that sort of thing. I'd hardly gone on a few dates, let alone shack up with anyone. I decided to drop it and let them believe what they wanted. They were going to punish me regardless… no cell phone, no games, and no friends.

"Where is Gina?" I asked.

"We sent your sister to stay at Nonna's house. We didn't know if you were in a ditch rotting somewhere and we didn't want her home when the police came to tell us you choked to death on your own putrid vomit." My dad had an aggressive way with words that I loved about him.

I went to back to my room to gather my thoughts. Nothing was how I left it. I was so tired the night before I hadn't realized that my room was cleaned and organized. The golden yellow walls had been wiped down and stripped of the various movie posters I'd collected. My dirty clothes had been washed and folded nicely into my dark red dresser. My room used to not smell... I mean, I'm sure it smelled, but it smelled like me; a fantastic mixture of cheap body spray and sweat. Now it smelled like vanilla soap.

I wasn't a messy guy but I wasn't a neat freak either and the amount of precision of organization meant that my dad was in here. I could just picture him, snooping around, looking under my mattress and through my drawers for any kind of clue as to where I was at. Part of me wished I had some ambiguous old note that said, "Be home later" from another date that he could have found with a chuckle.

Honestly, I was more relieved that I gave Cody back his stack of magazines that I had stashed in the bottom of a large black footlocker at the foot of my bed. I'm sure my parents figured I had become informed about the birds and the bees through school or TV, but we never officially talked about it and I'm not sure the given circumstance would have been the best. Then again, my dad already thought I was with a girl for these missing three weeks, so I'm sure he knows I know.

I stood there, staring blankly at the large window that looked out into my backyard. Our house was on the edge of a creek line that led to a nearby man-made lake. The area was undeveloped and wooded. So much of my childhood was spent exploring the nooks and various treasures abandoned. Large tractor tires and giant blocks of Styrofoam made their way up from the lake by floating in the flooding seasons. I used to think it was so cool.

The adventure beyond my window seemed so long ago and far less complicated than the traveling in the Furtherland. Of course, this world had its own dangers too. I was always wary of wild animals until one managed to cross my path, then I had the determination to contact it with all the failure one might expect from domesticating the wild. It's odd that I'd done such a poor job of catching or taming any of the squirrels or rabbits I'd often chased down, yet, managed to capture and keep Virgil as a somewhat disciplined pet in the other world.

"What the Hell is your problem?" Tony stormed into my room, shoving me onto the bed.

"What's your problem?" I retaliated.   .

"Don't give me any of that bull about being with some chick. I know you're making up some piss poor explanation. Where were you?"

"I…" I couldn't think.

"Where were you, Dom? So help me, if you don't give me a straight answer I will destroy you." Tony said, holding me down. His face snarled as he spit the words at me. I knew he wasn't playing.

"I can't explain" I choked out under Tony's weight.
"After all the stuff with mom! After all I've done for you! You are more a selfish whining bastard now than you've ever been." His words cut deep.

"What am I supposed to say? I went to some magical world with monsters and Indians." I could tell my retort took him off guard. I'm sure of all the things he expected me to say that was not one of them.

"Just tell me the truth." Tony pleaded.

"Okay. I acquiesced. "You aren't going to believe it, but okay."

I told him what had happened… about the attic, and the monster, the oval town, and even the Whoez. He stared at my bruised face and body, trying to reconcile the words he was hearing with the damage he could see. At one point he stared so hard into my pupils I was certain he was checking to see if I was intoxicated. Needless to say, he was not impressed with my story. I know he didn't believe it, but I think he could tell I wasn't lying either, which made him quiet and very troubled. I knew the way he looked at me with burning anger and compassion. That sad, broken hearted stare I've seen on his and my dad's face before, none more distraught than my dad's, and I knew what he was thinking…

I was going crazy just like my mother.

Chapter 11:
The Beautiful Emptiness

"I have to tell dad..." Tony said in somber admission. "You're sounding like Mom."

"I'm not!" I shouted. "I'm nothing like her. You just don't understand. I don't understand."

"Then show me" Tony demanded.

"Show you what?" I cried.

"Show me how you went to this magical No-Freakin-Way land. I want to see for myself."

"I don't know if it will work again. I didn't mean to do it the first time and honestly, I have no idea how I got back."

"What a colorful pile of crap. I have two options... Either I believe you're lying to me for no good reason, or you are in desperate need of help."

"I..." I stopped, Tony waited. "I'll show you. Just let me get dressed first."

★★★★★

Ten minutes later we met at the staircase leading to the attic. Tony was a step ahead when he tripped where the stairs dipped. We both stopped as he regained his composure. It was an awkward moment, and I laughed a little but Tony was in no mood. Neither of us were talking. I was terrified. What if he was right? What if I was like my mother?

Something inside me wanted to turn and run. It was what I was good at and seemed to be the answer more often than not. Running got me out of a lot of trouble in the past, but I was certain Tony would be behind me, step for step, with an unmatched determination. So we pressed on, past the window where the Murphys were washing their boat, as they often did in the summer.

We reached the attic and pressed on the ceiling where the stairs touched. Tony stopped and motioned for me to go in first, so I did. I stood up and grabbed the string on the light, bringing the entire room alive with light with a quick click. Tony put his head up and watched.

"So what did you do?" he asked.

"I just hopped on the beams and was about to leave when..."

"Try to do it again." He said.

I tried following the path I took as close as I could, making my way all the way to the window where the faceless mirror stood. I pushed the mirror aside. Nothing was happening, which is what we both expected. Tony shook his head in disappointment and began down the steps.

"Tony, wait!" I shouted running after him. A gust of wind rushed into the attic pressing me forward when

Tony's head popped back up in response to my call. The wind whistled loud and created a vacuum which pulled me back just as hard as it had just pushed me forward. The unbalanced air broke my stride, causing my foot to miss one of the beams and suddenly I was falling through the drywall ceiling that hung underneath the unfinished attic floor.

Everything shattered.

★★★★★

When my eyes adjusted enough, I saw I was now in a far corner of some lightly wooded area near fruit bearing trees. It took me a few minutes to realize I'd traveled back into the Furtherland. I came to this conclusion after watching the sky for a few minutes shift in color before passing one of Oo-Phoo's clouds. It was a horse, similar to the first one I'd seen in the Furtherland, but now rearing up rather than darting forward. His art truly was magnificent.

The world was open. One direction led to a mountain I was certain I had not been to. Another led further into the orchard. The last visible course was a hill ridden path, which was considerably more practical to navigate than the others. I didn't recognize where I was, so I chose the direction of the hills and began walking.

I lost count of the hours that passed. My mind thinking over all the time I spent back at home and what my family would think now that I was gone again. Did Tony see me transition between the worlds, breaking through the invisible threshold? How long will I be gone this time? Or worse yet, have I gone crazy like my mother and this was somehow the only way my mind could reconcile what it desperately wanted to not be true.

The thoughts were weighing on me as it seemed like I'd been walking for days when I noticed the hills ended at what appeared to be the end of the world. There it was, an impassable wall of lush green vines so thick and high it was impossible to go through or over. Each one was woven into a beautiful thick rope that connected to the next, and then the next, and so on. Small thorns seemed to grow bigger as the wall grew taller. It only took a glance to realize that climbing was out of the question. However, it seemed altogether possible to snake my way through the brush. After a few attempts to push through, my hand had become tangled.

Immediately my mind went into a panic.

I can't say if the vines were trying to take hold of me though I wouldn't be surprised if they did, but the more I struggled to break free, the more tangled I became, first from my hand, then to my wrist, and all the way up to my elbow. The entire event occurred in just seconds, but somehow, after several frightening moments of struggling, I had freed myself. Attempting to find my way through seemed nearly impossible and possibly suicidal. I decided to follow the wall and hope for a break, and a break is what I found.

About a mile or so from where I had been tangled was a narrow, high stretching archway that came to a point at the top. It appeared as though someone had unzipped the wall of vines as there was no stone or rock to support such a monstrous thing. The vine archway led into a narrow tunnel that lead to nothing. You may assume by nothing I mean a wall of more vines, or some vast darkness, but I don't mean the dark abyss of space. I mean nothing the way that a blank canvas has nothing drawn on it. Space, stretching in every direction towards infinity, was empty. The vine tunnel ended as though I was standing on the cliff of existence, ready to travel into the next world. The vision of nothing was somehow the most beautiful and strange thing I'd ever seen. So many possibilities and potential for unused reality and yet, there it was... emptiness.

I thought maybe I'd be able to step off and float like in outer space, so I kicked the ground a bit, breaking off a tiny bit of dirt and tossed it in to see if it would suspend in the alabaster void. The dirt didn't float but evaporated with a terribly unsettling squeal. I may have been the first person ever to kill dirt.

Entering the beautiful emptiness seemed impossible until I saw a figure walking on an invisible path just a tad higher in elevation than I had been. It was a woman; A long, tall, vaguely alien with pointy features, but unmistakably a beautiful woman. She had long white hair which hung as an arrangement of thick feathers. Her hands and feet were sharpened claws that bore shiny pearl scales. She had black soulless eyes, obsidian lips, and what can only be described as enough clothing to cover a small portion of her top half. If I hadn't just seen the dirt dissolve and curse me with its final breath, I may have jumped in myself. She was stunning!

She stopped a few feet away, still on a higher platform of elevation, stooped, squinted and asked me with disgust, "What are you?"

"I'm a man." I screeched out, sounding far less confident than intended.

"What's a man made of?" she continued skeptically.

I thought for a moment then said, "I supposed the same thing you are, just arranged a little different."

"I doubt it. Why don't you come here so Non-Shah can see you better..." she said shifting her tone from arrogant skepticism to menacing.

"I think I'll stay here." I said shakily.

Her tone shifted again, this time to a patronizing pout. "Oh, are you scared? What's the worst that can happen?"

"I'm almost certain I just saw dirt die... I'm pretty sure it's not safe for me to cross into there."

"So, what! You saw dirt die. Are you made of dirt?"
"No... I'm a man." I responded angrily.
"I doubt it." she mocked.

The conversation had come full circle and she was getting me more aggravated by the moment. I wanted to find her repulsive, but she was erotic in poise and appearance. She was beautiful.

I stood there for an awkward minute and stared at her. She sat with her legs dangling off the edge of the invisible platform she was on and made gruesome faces at me. Then her eye's brightened. She decided to take off her top and with a flirty twirl motioned for me to enter.

I restrained myself the best I could, but came dangerously close to the edge, burning off a small portion of skin on my hand. The pain confirmed what I had guessed. She was trying to lure me in to kill me. Worse yet, was admitting that her death was where I wanted to be. I was alone, with my private destruction mere inches from my face. Lust was luring me. In a moment, it would all be over and no one would know what happened.

"Are you trying to kill me?!" I yelled, holding my hand.

She didn't answer with words… instead, she shouted wildly and threw her clothes down at me…

They smelled really good…

Again, I restrained myself from jumping in, but luckily for me, her feral cries and spastic movements were more off-putting than attractive. The spell I found myself under had ceased long enough for me to decide to leave. I turned back and left through the tunnel of vines in a daze.

I'm not sure what actually occurred in that vine tunnel, but I was convinced… Non-Shah is crazy.

Tony's Letter:

Hey Dom,

What the hell did I just see? Where did you go? One minute you're tripping, you fall through the attic floor and you're gone. YOU ARE GONE!

HOW? How in the world is that even possible? That is some serious Houdini stuff.

I'm not an idiot. I still don't believe your stories... Your myths and monsters don't make any sense. I really don't know what to believe, but certainly not my lying eyes.

Just so we're on the same page I made up a story for mom and dad. I couldn't say what I saw, that's for sure. Even if it was true, who'd believe me? Maybe mom, but definitely not dad, and if mom believed me, she'd probably move into the attic until you came back.

I told them some girl came by and you ran off. As for the attic floor... well, let's say you owe me big. I told mom and dad I was the one who fell through bringing some stuff up there.

I don't know where you are or when you are coming back, but when you do, you better call me. We have some reality to straighten out.

-Tony

Chapter 12:
Children of Shame

When I left the beautiful emptiness, I decided to trace my steps back towards the direction the clouds were being made. The idea wasn't half bad, as a few hours later I knew where I was.

This once wide and foreign world was starting to become smaller, more manageable and familiar. I no longer wandered aimlessly from location to location but began recognizing paths and landmarks which became more revealing than street signs I'd often taken for granted. With so much of this world being alien to me, I was grateful that the portions I encountered were at least consistent. A world this odd could have easily warped, rearranging landscapes and physics, and I'd have known no difference. However, the Furtherland, as strange as it was, was knowable and for the moment that was comforting.

I found the clearing just before the Ashwoods and planned to enter when a large puff of smoke rose into the air, exchanging elevation for substance, as the former cloud came in to settle. A new hour passed and Oo-Phoo would soon be coming out and I decided to meet him there. I made my way to where the trees lay inward creating a bridge over the ash-covered ground. He stumbled out, looking more disheveled than before. I wanted to help him, but I knew I couldn't and I was certain he wouldn't accept my help even if I were capable. Neither he nor I would be able to change the desire that welled in us.

"Hi Oo-Phoo..." I called out.

I can't be certain he heard me. He slumped along, with his bowlegged stride, passing by me with not so much as a glance still chanting his work ballad... "All day, every day, every single hour. Never a break, always awake. Every minute soured.".

"Oo-Phoo! Wait up!"

I had no trouble following the burly ape-like man. His speed on land was far less sensational than his impressive log navigation. I had half a mind to travel ahead of him when I noticed the path carved out in the brush which appeared to be created by the constant wear of his obsessive patrol. Still, I resisted, following close behind him into an orchard. The treetop was not nearly as heavy as the Ashwood's canopy, however, was arguably more stunning. The trees were erupting in bold, warm colors, mimicking the wilting autumn reds and oranges but with lush, vibrant life. The leaves rattled in the wind, creating the illusion that the orchard was set ablaze. The only contrast was the enormous flowers shaped like bells hanging down from the branches, which retained the deep black sheen or an oil slick, with all the marbled colors swirling.

Oo-Phoo reached the stump of a tree with a large heavy ax resting against it. I stopped at a distance expecting the muscle built man to demonstrate impressive chopping, especially as he took hold of the ax. Then, without drawing his arm back but a few inches from the trunk he smacked the ax against a tree with the flat side. The impact made a loud *CRACK* and sent birds and bugs into flight. The hit was unsuccessful it seemed. Oo-Phoo was understandably tired and it seemed as though I may be witness to the end of a long period of time keeping.

The trees again became aroused, as though a second wave of birds was late to their sudden exodus. I looked up and was met with something unexpected. Within the foliage was a guy. It's hard to say how old exactly but he appeared to be my age, maybe a bit older. The guy was not dressed in the fine raiment that the people in the town wore. Instead, he wore pelts, leather, and bone armor, far more traditional to the Native American's of the world I was familiar with. Or at least, some period of time from the world I was familiar with. He dropped down 2 large fruits into Oo-Phoo's arms. With a sudden jerk and a wince of pain, Oo-Phoo turned and returned down his path towards the tree.

"Hey" I called out.

"Hey-Yo... Oh!" called the voice from the tree with a sense of astonishment.

"Why do you sound surprised?"

"Could be that I haven't talked to anyone but my father for ages. Could be because you're white as a cloud."

"I guess I can't argue that. I'm Dominick."

"Shikoba" He tapped the side of a tomahawk to his chest indicating his name. "So, dad, when did you start making friends? I thought this job was too important to do anything else."

Oo-Phoo kept down the path, hardly twitching as the question offensively caught his ears.

"So you've been helping your dad with this?"

"I suppose you can call it helping. I'd say I was stuck doing this because he felt he had something to prove. Let me ask you something... You've been to the town, right?"

"Yeah..."

"Does anyone even look at the clouds anymore?"

"Yeah... I think. I mean, I saw them look up a few times."

"See, they all probably think we're a couple of idiots." Shikoba shouted over my shoulder at his dad.

"Why don't you stop then?" I asked.

"I can't. My father is stuck in this loop of cloud making and can't help himself anymore. Our people are to respect and obey our parents even when they lead us into absurdity like this. Yeah, it's hard to see him suffer this way... trapped in an endless circuit, wandering back and forth, always moving away from one problem only to be walking towards the next and never going anywhere. To leave him when he's clearly not well would be a worse offense than to assist."

"Do you have a mom or siblings? Maybe you can take turns."

"They're back at the town. I thought I was being noble. I thought I would be seen as a hero. For a time they would visit and bring food... now it's just my father and me, a tree short of a few leafs, sleeping and eating outside when we can take a break. I've never been so ashamed of my blood. I wish I could bleed out every last drop and become something else."

"Oh man. I'm sorry to hear that. Is there anything I can do to help? Maybe I could do a few runs with the fruit to give your father and you an honest rest."

"If only I could accept that offer. However, my father wouldn't give you the chance to fail him. I once tried to take over for him… apparently I was not as fast as he'd liked and my cloud carving wasn't up to his standard. So now he only trusts me to help him get these fruit to use. Even then he argues with the size of the fruit."

"Wow. I thought your dad was a smart guy too."

"Oh, he is smart. He seems to know more about this place than anyone else. The Furtherland is still a strange place to most of us, but dad took to this world and hardly remembers the old world. It's especially hard to argue with him when he seems to be right all the time."

"Maybe your dad has a serious mental disorder."

"I'm not sure if I follow."

"I don't want to sound rude, but it happens sometimes. When I was about 12, my mother went through a severe episode of depression. She started to slow down in her thinking, like she couldn't process any information. She had to leave her job. For weeks, she would sit on the living room couch and stare. She wouldn't even bother to put on the light, My dad hated it and often tried to help her. Sometimes she'd even admit she needed help. She cried a lot. My mother and I used to be so close and I wanted to hug her and help her, but she pushed me away. My dad became so angry at her. Looking back, I could tell it must have been awfully hard on their marriage.

This went on for months until one day I had accidentally broken the glass on the face of an antique grandfather clock we kept in the hallway. My mother was home, but dad was at work. I don't even remember what I did to break it. The glass shattered in, jamming the gears. Something about the loud crash roused her from her catatonic composure. She jumped up to examine the clock, a gift her late father had given to her. When she'd seen the extent of the damage she pounced on me like a feral animal.

She started beating me... Actually beating me; in a closed fisted fury. The glass had embedded into her hand, cutting me over and over with each strike. I was so afraid; I thought she was going to kill me. Her blank stare had curled to regret as though she'd actually made up her mind to do so; like she had no choice. She might have done it if it weren't for my older brother coming home when he did. Tony heard my screams from outside, ran into the house and knocked my mother down. He held her as best he could and told me to run, so I ran. I remember my mother storming out the house, chasing me down the street, calling for me to come back and pleas of being sorry. I kept running. I was terrified. I was heartbroken. I didn't know where to go so I ended up at a nearby park where I climbed up and hid at the top of a slide.

Later that night my dad drove around calling out for me. When I heard his voice I ran to him crying and he took me home. When I got home, my mother was packing. Tony told dad what had happened. My mother told dad what happened. I went to my room and hid. There was hardly a reason for me to say anything. Within the next few hours my mother was taken to a behavioral hospital. Over the next months she was placed on various medications and examined until she was deemed regulated and fit to come home. Things between my mother and I were sour for a long time... they still are, and my dad is doing all he can to get things to feel normal again."

"I'm sorry..." Shikoba said with genuine sympathy.

"We all need a little help sometimes."

"What should I do then? Do you think my dad will hurt me?"

"I don't know if I can offer any advice on what you can do with your dad. In my world, doctors would help. Here, I don't know what can be done."

The air became tense. Shikoba seemed to be lost in a deep pause, taking random hacks at the tree with his hatchet as if he were chopping the overgrown brush of weary thoughts. "Did you ever forgive her?"

"...Yeah." I paused before replying. The truth was I hadn't spent much time with mother since then. In fact, most of the time I was home, which was rare in of itself, was spent keeping Gina away from mom. "I'm sorry to put this all on you. I rarely ever talk about it anymore, but I thought…"

"No… you didn't." He interrupted. "I knew my dad wasn't quite right, but maybe I've been shielding from myself the severity of the situation. You've given me a lot to think about…"

"Okay." I said, partially ashamed that I brought it up, and more so upset I didn't have answers for Shikoba. I stood for a while. A deafening wind breaking the silence with a chilling rattle of the thick leaves on the tree and howling through the bell-shaped flowers. "I think I'm going to head back to town." Shikoba nodded.

Chapter 13:

Dream Catcher

I spent the day in the town, watching the people work; making food, eating food, and of course drinking that dark red wine. Again I was invited to stay at Nock's home, but this time I wasn't as modest as I had been the meal before, having more than I should. They could tell I wasn't able to hold the wine as well as they could and offered me Makya's bed to stay in. It was stiff, but after a strong drink and the constant back and forth of warping between worlds, I passed out in no time.

★★★★

I was rattled awake by a violent shaking.

"Get up." Aeya beckoned with a raspy whisper.

"Why? Is everything okay?"

"I want to take you to the towers."

"Okay…" I struggled to wake myself up. "Why are we whispering?"

"Shhhh… It's a secret." She said with a smile. "Meet me outside." She called as she left the room. I could hear her on the other side of the wall whispering to someone else.

"Is he coming?"

"Yeah."

"Did you explain it to him?"

"Not yet."

I put my shoes and hoodie on, neither of which I remembered taking off, and met Aeya and Vaesti outside.

"Hey Vaesti."

"Glad you're coming. Let's go." Commanded Vaesti with urgency.

We weren't a hundred yards away when Makya also joined us with a rod in his hand. None of Nock's children said a thing, so neither did I.

We continued to walk for miles. Aeya shoved me and ran. I caught my footing and sprung towards her. Makya stuck his stick out, causing me to trip.

"You're dead!" I shouted, taking off at the two running for their lives. I caught Makya first, who crowed in victory as I tackled the boy.

"Hey!" Aeya shouted.

"Oh, you still want some?" I stood and once again took off after the girl. She crowed and I raced hard. I could tell she was really trying to escape, but it wasn't long until I caught her as well. "Gotcha!" I bragged, tagging her on the shoulder. She yelped with a smile. Vaesti watched and giggled with a loud snort. We all laughed

We chased one another across the flat land, until it tapered off into a desert of glass. It was then I could see the blue silhouette of the abandoned city I saw from the top of the cliff, as they were obscured through layers of atmosphere. They were transparent then, like precious diamonds, but as we got closer the sky became thick like a dense milky fog. The wilderness was absent in that circle of enormous crystals structures; No trees, no grass, no creatures of any sort. A silent city disturbed only by an ominously hollow hum.

"That's where the Sabanora comes from" Makya pointed to as we approached.   And just like I remembered, I could see the light erupting from crystal towers as I had the day I first arrived.

"It's cool. Is that why we're here?"

"We are going to see Iktomi." Vaesti spoke with excitement.

"Underneath the towers lives a creep named Iktomi." Said Aeya

"You must be very careful of Iktomi as he is deals in dreams. He is always in a state of creating and repairing his snare. This snare filters the worlds, sorting the good and the bad, catching dreams." Makya grunted in disapproval.

"So is this place the good or bad stuff?" I puzzled.

"Both... Good, bad, and all varying degrees. It's life." Aeya smiled with clarity.

We found our way through the fog to find an intricate threading woven from transparent fibers into an enormous web between the towers. We all stared up in wonder. Pearls of varied sizes clung, fixed to the silver lace.

"What are those pearls?" I asked in awe.

"Dreams..." Aeya replied with the same tone of awe.

All at once we shot our glance to a single corner as something red moved rapidly along the web. Makya pulled out a hand full of disks , to which Aeya motioned to put them away. Down the wire crawled a creature with the body of a very slender man, no more than 4 feet tall, and shrouded in a thick deep red robe. When he arrived I was startled by his deathly green skin and devil red pupil eyes. He smiled with a mouth full of tiny fangs which he ran his black tongue over..

"Welcome back Aeya. I see you brought some friends." Iktomi slurped.

"You came here already?" Vaesti asked, showing great concern for her sister.

"How's that dream working for you?" Iktomi teased. Aeya ignored the taunt. "What can I do for you today?" The creature scanned the crowd of us, still licking his sharp teeth.

"You can capture dreams. Can you bring people back that have gone?" Vaesti asked anxiously.

"I'm sorry. I think you might have confused my talents. I make the web. The web catches the dreams... but if there's something else I can help with..." Iktomi reached his long fingered hands to touch Vaesti, but was smacked by Makya's staff before he could make contact. "Aaah!" he roared in pain. Makya smiled and I couldn't help smirking too.

"So, have you come for a good reason or just to watch the child hurt me."

"Can you tell me who the Whoez is?" I blurted out.

"Never heard of him." Iktomi quickly replied. "Anything else?"

"Why am I here? What keeps bringing me to this place?"

"Now that is something I do know…" Iktomi climbed back up the web, crawling from fiber to fiber, picking up a pearl. "I've seen the dreams of a woman who chases you." His beady eyes continued to shift around the group.

"She did this?" I said, thinking of my mother.

"Don't be so dramatic. You are where you want to be. The greater question you should be asking is what brought you back home?"

I thought of my family. Of my dad, and Tony, and Gina. How much I wished things were normal.

"What is it you dream of Vaesti? Is it a boy? No... My pardon, it's a man! Tuk-Rah the brave warrior."

"Where is he? Is he okay?" Vaesti pleaded.

"I haven't seen his dreams in some time, but I'm sure he's around. And what of the boy. What do you dream of Makya?" Iktomi pulled himself to another level of his web and looked deep into a pearl. "Of course. The boy dreams of his ill fated mother." Iktomi patronized the child. "Do you miss her?"

"I know what I dream of." Makya dismissed the guile of Iktomi's ridicule. "What can you tell me that I don't know?"

"Alright. I've been a bit cruel." Weaseled the little man. "It's true I know your fondest dreams and I've seen your deepest nightmares. Each of you are afraid of what already happened and what it says about you. That you've failed. I can make those dreams go away."

"You can do that?" I asked with skepticism.

"All you have to do is come into my web." He slurred on a mouthful of saliva, licking his fangs even faster. I took a step forward only to be whacked by Makya's rod.

"Don't!" Makya warned. "He intends to eat you."

"You're no fun." Pouted the creep.

"Let's go. There isn't anything for us here anymore." Aeya pulled.

"So long. Oh, and Dominick... Be careful whose dreams you are a part of." Iktomi warned with devilish grin.

Chapter 14:

The Dimming

When we returned to the town Nock's children assimilated back into the busy society, returning to work like everyone else who'd woken from their nap. I wanted to help, but didn't know where to begin, which lead to me wandering around towards the graveyard. The graveyard was the strangest I'd seen. It almost had the feel of a war memorial the way the stones were all uniform in cut, color, and material, planted in rows more precise than the crops over my shoulder.

All the stones had strange symbols engraved on them, similar to those on the houses roofs. I walked on a small path down the center, hoping that I wasn't somehow being disrespectful to these people by visiting their dead. There was only one stone out of place.

It was the same size and cut, but the material seemed to be some sort of sapphire, fixed into the ground with a silver setting which wrapped around the edges in fantastic intricacies. The appearance resembled expensive jewelry, almost like an engagement ring. It glowed with intense purpose, much brighter than the street lights in the town. This blue headstone had no symbol engraved, rather had writing.

The gravestone read:

Armour Grave

I puzzled at the meaning for a few moments. Makya, seeing me confused, came down the path and met me at the sapphire stone. I didn't know what to say at first. He was a pretty quiet kid; nothing like his father, Nock.

"Hey, Makya. What is this?"

"That's the Armour Grave."

"Yeah?" I touched the metal setting on the engraved stone.

We both stared at the stone a moment when Makya continued. "My dad once said something was growing in there."

"Growing? You mean something alive is buried here?" I asked.

"I suppose."

"And it's just in there? Why would something alive be buried? Seems like the most inhumane thing to do."

"I don't know. Maybe because things don't die in graves?" Makya pressed his ear against the stone, listening intently. "If it isn't dead, whatever is in there must be sleeping. As long as it stays asleep, what difference does it make?"

"But what if it wakes up?" The words escaped more concerned than I intended. You'd think with the heavy breath I argued, there would have been something urgent provoking me, but there wasn't.

"Maybe that's what the setting is for. To keep it in."

"What if the Armour Grave is to keep something out?" I returned.

"Then it's best you leave it alone. Don't go digging up graves... Especially ones named 'scary eyes'."

Minutes stretched... I searched my thoughts for something to break an uncomfortable pause.

"Can you kill the Whoez?" I asked him.

"I suppose. I haven't met anything I couldn't kill, but I haven't tried to kill everything I've met." Makya replied as though the question about premeditated murder was no different than killing a thanksgiving turkey.

"Should I kill the Whoez?" I asked sternly.

"If you think you have to. It's hard to stand behind something you don't believe in but it's even harder to not stand on something that you do. I don't see a point of it, but that's your decision to make.

We walked back to the town.

★★★★★

The hour clouds never blocked the missing luster of an absent sun. Shadows hardly existed, except for the brief moments between the dancing glow of the living light. I had come to know this, expect it even, and was completely comfortable with the unchanged brightness swaying between wonderful calming shades. That was until the sky became stuck on pink for a few seconds too long... I hardly noticed when the color cycle refused to change, then something even stranger happened. The sky itself seemed to close in, adopting the most unsettling crimson tone. The devil sky darkened. The Sabanora had retreated to the ground and hid. Light began to dim and vanish, turning the standing objects into silhouette before the shadow engulfed everything. The diamond street lamps maintained their eerie glow, confirming that the light had in fact been trapped in them. The town's people began to howl and shake with fear. It wasn't dark often in the Furtherland, but it was clear that when it was the people were instantly aware and terribly afraid.

Was this a storm? Or perhaps the Whoez had become responsible for the changing world in his effort to draw me out and kill me. I was not as scared as I was angry at this thought. I wanted to charge into the open fields and call out to the wind in defiance to make my stand and let it be known that I was ready for battle.

A soft hand had grabbed mine. It was Aeya. She seemed concerned, afraid even, but she was brave and not moaning like the rest of the people. I adored that about her. I had half a mind to grab her into my arms and hold her until the horror ended. "What if it doesn't end?" I thought. "What if this is the moment I needed to prove myself?" I caressed her face gently, making a silent promise to come back for her. I charged down the cobblestone path into the wild…

I looked out towards the cloud maker, Oo-Phoo, to see that the Ashwoods were no longer birthing smoke, but fire. Fire filled these skies, still in the designated time slot, traveling along that familiar path. No more, and no less light came from it.

A luring figure emerged from over hill opposite from behind where I was facing. Had it not been for a curious sense of being watched, I would never have turned in time.

It was Piop. His eyes were vacant with rabid lust. His mouth, glossy with hunger, curled ferociously revealing rows of jagged teeth. There was no soul in the monster now that he had become hungry. What he wanted was meat and any source was as good as the next.

I stood 25 yards from him, unsure if this was going to be a chase or a showdown. I didn't need to make the decision, as the moment Piop lunged forward I began running opposite. The monster used its long arms to propel itself forward, almost like a racing gorilla. Still, I was much faster than Piop. Yet, without anywhere in particular to go other than running circles, it was a mere moment before he was closing in behind me. I had to come up with a plan fast. I could probably trick it into the emptiness to have a date with crazy Non-Shah, but that path was long and far from where we were. I was getting tired and knew I couldn't maintain my thin lead ahead. He was clearly determined to chase me as long as it would take. I decided to lead him into the dense emergent, thinking he may slow down or get stuck in the thick wet mud. At this point, I was hoping he'd either find something else to eat or do something clumsy enough to hurt himself for me to get free.

It was then I saw the Whoez, crouched on one of the long angled logs that jutted from woven roots in the marsh. I imagined the Whoez laughing at how ridiculous the chase must have looked to him. I had two problems. Thoughts darted in my mind and the only conclusion I could make was to get Piop and the Whoez to somehow chase one another. I ran towards the Whoez screaming like a mad man. I slid underneath the tree as close to the trunk as I could fit through. Piop, distracted by the sight of new food, lunged wildly at the tree to make the Whoez his new lunch. In an instant, the Whoez had unsheathed his sword and lobbed off Piop's hand at the thin forearm. The monster fell and writhed in pain. Then almost as if he had come to his senses he began calling out to me.

"Dominick, help me! Please, I don't know where I am!"

My heart nearly broke. He must have been in some hunger trance and couldn't get out. He probably battled his hunger the entire chase, holding back what sense of self he had just so I could escape. I paused, my heart breaking from wanting to help him but maintaining caution. He clawed forward in the muddy grass with his remaining hand, looking for a way to pull himself up. I looked at the Whoez, still perched atop the limbless tree, whose fractured mask had turned between the monster and the sky, almost drawing some correlation between the two. I abandoned reason and took a few steps closer. The Whoez, reached into his overcoat pulling out a clenched fist. It was clear he was holding something though it took me a moment to realize what; Discs.

The monster continued dragging himself in pain, looking back at the Whoez with his own fear. He shouted.

"Stay away! No… Leave me alone!"

He knew he was going to die. Suddenly I knew it too. I darted towards him in a full sprint, picking up a rock on the way. Then, as if all occurring in unison, the Whoez threw the discs, I threw the rock, and the monster curled its lips in anger.

WHHHHhhhhheeeeeeeeeeeee…. Pft.

The discs went through Piop's head; all of them. Clean holes, allowing rivers of blood to spill out.

The rock I'd thrown hit the Whoez in the leg, knocking him off his perch; though I was aiming for his head. He stood holding himself, revealing he was truly hurt. I paused for a moment to look back at Piop, his body flat on the ground. The rage welled up in me and I turned to chase the Whoez.

Despite being hurt, the Whoez ran with an unsettlingly twisted limp. I chased and was closing in. We went over the hill, through the wet grass, down to the water bank, and when I was one step behind him, he dove into the murky water and disappeared. I thrashed at the waves looking but couldn't find anything. Any other time the water would have been milky white with a vibrant glow, showing all the fish and creatures moving within, but for the moment, in the dark only splinters of light bounced off the surface for a moment before disappearing. I waited maybe a half an hour, never seeing the Whoez surface. Either he knew of some underwater tunnel or had an incredible ability to hold his breath. Regardless, I was certain he was not dead.

Chapter 15:

The Unmasking

—•⚜—

The sky slowly returned to its usual shifting tones. I arrived back at the oval town, not speaking or making eye contact with anyone. Instead, I went directly to the windmill to grab a shovel and then returned to the marsh to bury Piop's body. I didn't know him much, but I felt he deserved some form of dignity. When I returned, parts of his body had been missing as though an animal had picked off a few scraps before running deeper into the wild. I buried the beast, said a prayer, and traveled once again back to the town.

All the people had returned to their business as though nothing had happened, moving in a choreographed routine like ants returning to work after a heavy rain. I entered Nock's home to find Aeya entertaining a small child by playing a strange stringed instrument I could only liken to a violin. She held one piece between her shoulder and head while slowly pulling a bow across the face of the cords. She held a white cloth in the hand holding the neck of the instrument as if to perfect the grip. The notes were done with such precision and care humming enchantments as though it were the charmed song of a foreign voice. The Sabanora danced to her tune as if coming out of a long wintered hibernation, slowly rising, and then dispersing into the ambient sky.

"Did you compose this song?" I asked her

"What? Oh, not really. I mean, yes but I couldn't play it again. I'm not able to remember the music I play. I just do it and then it's gone."

"Wow. Well, I'm impressed. The song sounded sad. Are you okay?"

"Yes…" she said with false assurance. I could tell she didn't want to talk much about it and I thought maybe the dark sky reminded her of her mom.

"I'm sorry, Aeya. Do you know where I can find Makya."

"He's out getting dinner. You'll stay with us again, won't you?"

"I'm sorry, but I need to go."

"You're going to look for the Whoez, aren't you?"

"It looks like I don't have much of a choice. Do you have any of those discs your brother keeps? You know, just in case."

"No, Makya takes everything he uses with him… except the sword. He leaves my dad's old sword in the windmill behind the mirror in case something happens when he's out. It's a little too big and impractical for him to carry and use… yet anyway."

"A sword? Thanks! I'm probably going to need to borrow it."

"Hey, Dominick?" She called to me softly. "Did you ever love someone so bad you wanted them to die for not loving you?"

"No..." I puzzled before my thoughts landed on my mother.

She picked up my insecurity and sighed. "I'm scared for you Dominick. Fighting isn't always necessary in life... But if you absolutely have to fight, please fight for what is noble." Each word was spoken with a deep desire. I had the distinct impression she was concerned, possibly broken hearted over my suicide mission. She bit her lip and stared at me longingly. I was flattered, especially because she was incredibly pretty. If I had gone to school with her, I undoubtedly would have asked her to a dance or the movies. She was the kind of girl you wanted to put your jacket on to keep her from being cold. This budding relationship might be something to pursue in the future, but I realized that it wasn't what I wanted at that moment. I wanted blood.

With a gentle smile, I said goodbye then went to the windmill.

★★★★★

I climbed the stairs that stooped before climbing up to the loft and found a large two-edged sword resting behind the mirror. The sheath was leather with a phrase engraved...

"A sword by itself does nothing. The hand that holds it directs where it goes."

I've always loved the idea of a sword fight. The archaic battle seemed romantic and inevitable for the hero's last minute victory. Yet, as I was fitting the sword to my back, I realized the real danger. Choosing to hold a sword is not only a choice to hold your own life in your hands, but the lives of others as well. It's a strange feeling when you commit in your heart to killing someone. It's shocking and a bit scary to know that the plan from that moment forward is to take another person's life. I don't think I'll ever be able to shake that feeling.

I left the windmill and began walking towards the graveyard when I noticed the Whoez, standing atop the Armour Grave. I was so focused that I almost walked past without so much as a glance.

"I almost missed you" I shouted with confident anger.

"Some people hide in plain sight. Better be careful to not miss them." The Whoez hissed, standing up on the clearly still wounded leg with a challenging countenance. I squared my shoulders to face him.

"I'll give you a chance to walk away." I shouted, taking hold of the sword from the sheath on my back, second guessing my decision to fight.

The Whoez casually placed one hand on the sword he kept on his hip, hopped from the grave and walked towards me.

"At least tell me why you're doing this? Why wear a mask in a world so small that you couldn't possibly need to pretend to be anything."

"Would you rather I told you a hard truth or a comforting lie?" he hissed.

"The truth!" I insisted.

"This mask prevents war...The second face does not

portray a false nature but is a reminder of the inevitability of death. There is no delusion that this mask makes me something I am not. The way you saw me before was empty because the way you wanted to see me clouded your judgment of who I am. You hold prejudice against this face, as though the reminder of the ever looming death was offensive to only you."

It was then that the Whoez took off the mask. Behind the ivory plate was not the face of a man, but the face of a young woman. A face I'd seen before yet left me completely in awe. It was Aeya, but her feature appeared stronger now, more determined, resembling a Native American far more than they had before. Her skin was plain without makeup, wrinkled and sweaty from the mask but still incredibly pretty.

"Do you see it? Do you see my face now?" She called out to me in anger. "It's here, not hidden... not covered anymore. Does it make you uncomfortable? Is my face not what you wanted? "

"Yeah, I see you." I called back with angered confusion. "Why the Whoez? Why couldn't you leave well enough alone and just be you?" .

"This is me." She awkwardly chuckled. "I've been seeing you in my dreams for so long; always running. No matter how I chased you, you disappeared. Somehow you finally came to me... but then you shrugged me off as if you never knew me. You were here for the Whoez. That's what you were looking for in my world. So that's who I became for you. It's as though, in this mask you see yourself and find me to be more human, more alive, and more natural than the image you rejected behind it. Nothing has changed between us, not who I am, not who you are; but perhaps something has become more appealing, more palatable, more agreeable to eyes that only seek that which is most attractive."

"Is everyone crazy here? Your real face is nice. I might even say pretty if you weren't trying to kill me. You never gave me a chance to know you."

She lowered her head in the same manner as her reaction to my missed punch when she kicked me in the throat. I backed away. "You've had nothing but a chance to know me. This whole adventure you're on... was it not centered on the Whoez?"

I couldn't say anything. She was right. I've hardly thought about much of anything since arriving other than finding, avoiding, or warring against the Whoez. Here was my chance. She raised her head and unsheathed her sword before taking a step towards me. I knew the battle was coming.

Chapter 16:

'Til Death

There is no place in nature that fails at being an extraordinary setting for a final battle. The same is true for the Furtherland. Whether we were in the Ashwoods or the Dense Emergent, it wouldn't have mattered. But The Whoez found me here, in the short field between the graveyard and the windmill. Here we stood facing one another; all masks removed. Her eyes were stone. I knew she was stronger and it killed me. The rule I'd always known was that boys are stronger than girls. She didn't seem to mind breaking the rule. I found it difficult to not admire her.

"Do we need to do this?" I yelled out to her having second thoughts.

"You need to do this... I already know how this is going to end." She replied with unwavering determination.

"When this is over, it's over. There is no next time. I'm not going to chase you and fear you chasing me. One of us will have a free tomorrow." The frustration in my voice outweighed my attempt at being calm.

The first time we'd been in an altercation, she had me beat. I was confused, tired from the stairs, wounded from falling, and caught off guard. The second time I had her off guard and evened the score at 1 to 1. Now we were both prepared. This time, I knew this was going to be a dogfight, my pain from the fall had since numbed, and I was hoping the heavy stone I crushed her leg with still hurt enough to give me an edge. Speaking of edge, now I was holding a sword.

I liked the way that the sword fit in my hand. As I shuffled my hands for a tighter grip, the metal and leather underneath were cold. I felt powerful. My face must have gone mad with delight, like a child imagining himself a hero. I'm sure I've made the face a thousand times before, holding a stick high above my head, getting to whack my dad or my friend.

I stepped forward with a heavy chop, yelling "HIYAA!!"

It was at that moment I hesitated, realizing that the swing never went my way. She calmly stepped aside, making me fall on my own sword handle, whose blade stuck in the ground to give me a forceful punch in the stomach. It hurt a lot, but I knew I'd have to make this an advantage somehow. So I faked having the wind knocked out of me to gain the upper hand.

She took a few confident strides towards me. I abandoned the sword in the ground and spear tackled her. Coach would have been proud to see me. Her sword had left her hand upon impact and now she struggled under my weight. I felt her arm moving between our stomachs and I couldn't help but think she was going to stab me with some sort of hidden blade. I took a cheap shot while I had it and attempted to punch her in the face though she bridged her spine and my fist landed hard on her chest. She let out a gasp of air. I struggled to keep her down, but she grabbed my wrist and bent it in a horrifyingly unnatural way. I screamed in pain, and with that moment, she had clawed my face deep. I jumped off her holding my face. The wound opened, but the bleeding had afforded me a few last seconds before spilling out. I saw the instrument of her attack was on her hand, almost like a glove. It was Piop's claw.

I watched her stand, take her sword from the ground, and then readied herself. Enraged, I picked up a few cobblestones and threw them at her. My aim was lousy. Between my poor throwing and poor swinging, I began regretting not playing more baseball.

The fight was a joke. I had no chance. I tried doing the only thing I could think of, the only thing that worked so far. I ran to tackle her again...

We collided. The air filled with a pain-filled cry.

She won. She had stabbed me in the stomach. The sword still slotted in me prevented the blood from pouring out, but it dripped with anxious anticipation. I was disappointed but somehow satisfied that the battle was finally over.

"You got me. You win. You wore the mask, hid, and made me chase you... and now this. Was it all a sick game? Why did you do this to me?" I asked.

"I didn't want this. I didn't want to fight. From the beginning, this fight has all been you."

"Then what did you want?" I shouted.

"I wanted you!" she shouted and trailed off.

"Why?"

"I don't know. You seemed like someone I'd ... I don't know."

"You what? You love me? And that makes it okay for you to kill me? Where I come from love is supposed to give life, not death!"

"You're not dead. I'm almost certain I missed all the important parts." she said with an innocent smirk.

"Well, that's good." I said with a nervous chuckle, unsure of just how true that statement was. She chuckled back. It was a strange but incredibly sweet moment. The air poured over us and howled as though promising an oncoming storm. I could smell the rain in the approaching air though the water never came.

"Can you forgive me?" She said as her face dropped from a smile to near crying.

I'm not sure why but I felt bad for her; which is saying a lot, since I was skewered about a foot and a half through. But I wanted to forgive her more than anything else. I wanted to be done with resentment and grudges. I wanted to be free. I placed my hand on her face and assured her.

"Absolutely. I forgive you. Can you forgive me for hating you?" I confessed. She nodded. She wanted me to love her… and stranger still, I wanted to love and be loved by her. Death had become romantic again.

I don't know why I loved her so suddenly. Maybe I just wanted to love her. Thinking over each encounter with the Whoez I began to recognize the hatred I'd developed was merely a concoction I created from being unable to contain the mystery of something beyond strange in a strange place. I'd been told so many fairy tales that started and ended with the monster being the object of defeat that I rushed to assign that role to the first horrifying unknown I'd come upon.

I smiled at her through the hurt, unintentionally batting my eyes in a twitch reflex to the sharp pain shooting through my entire body. Truly, she was something. Then an untimely thought crossed my mind.

"Can I kiss you?"

She actually blushed at my request. Then she leaned in and kissed me hard. Her lips were soft and warm. She pressed against me just right. My whole body swelled with passion. I held her face in my hands. We smiled at one another and then she pulled the sword out.

Everything went black, and then suddenly I was falling.

Chapter 17:

Claw in Hand

I woke with the taste of blood in my mouth. Probably from coughing up what had found its way out of my veins into my open insides.

My eyes couldn't adjust. There was something on my face, some kind of blood-stained white cloth bandage. The light shone in from the window and for a moment I thought I was home. Then she came in... Aeya, the Whoez, dressed down and even more attractive than I'd seen her in her town clothes or as the Whoez. We were in the upper room in the windmill, just beautiful her and bloody me.

"What took you so long?" she chuckled.

"I'm sorry. It took me some time to come back to life after you killed me."

"I didn't kill you. I could never kill you." She said softly, stroking my scarred face with the claw.

"Ha, I could have killed you." I shot back, pushing the claw away.

"No, you couldn't. You think you could have, but literally, you had no chance." She smirked.

"How did you become the Whoez?"

"Do you remember Tuk-Rah, my sister Vaesti's love? My dad never liked him, but he was determined to win my father over. So, after what happened to my mother and father, Tuk-Rah was set out to kill the Stonecoats. But it was as my dad said we have rules and sent us out to stop him. For days we would find dead Stonecoats corpses scattered around the Furtherland, unfortunately, one day it was Tuk-Rah's body I found, his face, half peeled off, lying next to his final Stonecoat victim. They killed each other. I was grateful for what

Tuk-Rah did, even if it was wrong. Oddly, the murders brought peace. The Stonecoats learned about the scalped man they named "The Whoez" and stayed away from our town. It was in a moment of rash thinking I decided to do something radical. I hid Tuk-Rah's body and let the Stonecoats and Amank people believe the Whoez was still loose. Until then, there were only vague ramblings about the Whoez, so I created a disguise that covered enough to conceal my identity from my own people and hope that the chatter of a loose killer sighting would hold everything in order. Keeping everyone in suspense was easy. I'd venture out every so often. The Stonecoats stayed away and I never had to kill a single one. In time, I went back to Tuk-Rah's body to find he had decayed far beyond what I expected. This charade had gone too far and knew I could never convince the town that Tuk-Rah died since the Whoez was last seen. The truth is until I saved your life by killing your Stonecoat friend, I'd never killed one before."

"Wow..." I was shocked.

"I only wanted to do what was right."

I liked that Aeya was strong and nurturing; sweet and

snarky. Piop was right... As rushing water has the potential to soothe and corrode, so was the Whoez; a contradiction, in the most delicately dangerous way. No wonder it was so easy to love and hate her. Funnier still, my family was right; my trip into the Furtherland was about a girl.

"So what now? You finally got me. Am I your prisoner forever?"

"Now, I don't know what. I was hoping you could take me back with you."

"HA! I don't know how I'd explain you to my family. Hey mom and dad, I met someone in a mystical land, she's going to live with us now."

"Why couldn't that work? It would work with my family."

"Things are different here. There aren't social security numbers, birth certificate, education, and I'm sure a whole bunch of other things that would become a dead end for you if you came to my world."

"So everyone is numbered in your world?"

"Pretty much." I said with embarrassment.

"Okay... I'll be number 27." She joked. I smiled and shook my head. "So there's no way I can come there?" she asked. I again shook my head no. "Then you have to stay here."

"I don't think I can. My family was pretty sick about me being gone last time. Who knows how long it will seem this time. I can't just disappear on them. I love them."

"Don't you love me?" She went cold with doubt and pouted.

"I think I do... I mean, I do, but..."

"Here, in the Furtherland, when you love someone, you stay with them."

"I know... We do that in my world too, but I love my family. There's got to be a way to bring you home."

We sat for hours talking about options. Neither of us knew if she would be able to make it into my world. So far as I could tell, I was the only one who went back from the Furtherland and honestly, I had no idea how. Still, we couldn't help but entertain each thought as though each possibility was available to us.

I could visit... or she could, but that seemed hardly workable considering the time gaps between visits. I could leave my world behind, friends, family, school, all of it. It was strange how that seemed to even be an option. Still, it wasn't a reasonable option. She was willing to come with me, so I had to come up with a plan. That's when it occurred to me... she looked foreign. She was unfamiliar with American customs, and besides speaking fluent English, she maintained an accent that was just thick and strange enough to convince people she was foreign. She could be an immigrant. However, I knew immigration was becoming a big thing, and being deported to whatever fake country we'd say she belonged to was nearly worse than having her be a missing US citizen. That's what we decided she'd have to be a refugee. The story was set. We'd made our decision. She was coming home with me. The only problem was I had no idea how to get there.

"So how do we get to my world?" I asked her.

"I have no idea." She laughed. "Didn't you come here by yourself?"

"Are you serious!? I have no idea how I got here. I was convinced the Whoez was toying with me, dropping me between two worlds." I responded in shock.

"Maybe we can figure it out. What were you doing when you first came here?"

"I was in my attic both times when I came here."

"Okay, so how did you go back?"

"I honestly thought you brought me back right after our fight at the ruby stairs. You kicked me off of the cliff and I fell into my world."

"You didn't fall into your world. You fell into the water. I dragged you back to the windmill through the underground tunnel. I left you there, but when I came back you were gone."

"So what we know is that neither one of us intentionally did anything to get me here or send me back. In my world, the threshold is somewhere in my attic, but here... it might be in the windmill... which makes sense because they both have pieces of the mirror."

"The mirror? The mirror doesn't do anything."

We looked into it for a little while, waiting for something to happen. Nothing did.

"Did you say anything, or do anything to the mirror." she asked.

"No. I don't think I did anything to it. I was just there and the wind came in, and then there was a lot of light."

"The Sabanora did this?" she pondered.

"I didn't say that." I tried defending myself from sounding crazy.

"It's okay." she assured me. "The Sabanora is alive you know. I used to catch it in gems. It must have wanted to bring you here. Maybe the mirror isn't the method of transport but a sign of it; showing that these places are linked somehow."

"If they're linked, then why does the exit dump me somewhere nowhere by either my attic or the windmill?"

"I'm not sure. At least now we know that the threshold is somewhere between the two upper rooms."

We grabbed a few blocks and gems and brought it to the windmill hoping that their light would open this invisible gateway and whisk us both home. We waited and nothing happened. Our idea was failing, but we sat with one another. I had my back against the wall with the gears, facing the window on the opposite side while she lay between my legs, nestled. The Amank people seemed to love sleeping even more than we do.

★★★★★

A trumpet sounded loudly followed by the distinct rhythm of heavy unbalanced marching. The noise startled us to our feet. Aeya and I looked out the window and saw a hoard of Stonecoats curl from beyond the distant brush towards the town. The sky was not dark so we knew they were not coming for food. It was when we saw a gem encrusted coffin they carried with Piop's body that we realized the Stonecoats were coming for war.

A man I'd not seen yet rushed out to meet them at the main entrance of the town.

"Who is that?" I asked.

"That's Mizahn… He's our governor and Tuk-Rah's father."

Mizahn, made his way out to the Stonecoats, reaffirming the vast size difference between the two races. The Amank people vastly ranged in height but all within conventionally human ranges. The Stonecoats were all uniformly large, fat bodied creatures with thin limbs. Aeya and I held out breath to hear the conversation. Lucky for us both Mizahn and the Stonecoat leader were shouting.

"What's this about, Uwaht?" Mizahn called out firmly.

"Another Stonecoat brother has been slain. More of our blood spilt. Give us the Whoez, or we take your town." Uwaht, the Stonecoat commander, charged.

"The Whoez is not one of us. He's not here." Mizahn replied with stern defense.

"LIES! We know he is. We smell our brother Piop within your town. His blood is there." Uwaht insisted, pointing his large talon in Mizahn's face.

"That's impossible. The Whoez has fled from us. We've not known him since this matter began." Mizahn shouted back with restrained anger.

"Then let us in and we'll see for ourselves." Uwaht said with a motion, signaling the Stonecoat to commence the search.

The Stonecoat were brutal, tearing and clawing at every obstacle in their path, with noses twitching in impatient investigation. The people congregated at the center of the town, sobbing with restraint as their homes were raided. The Stonecoat knew what they were looking for... the missing claw, the one in Aeya's hand. The old woman in the town looked up into the windmill to see Aeya and I staring out the window into the pillaging. We both quickly crouched down. It wouldn't be long before they found us.

Aeya was an amazing fighter... Had the horde been only a handful of Stonecoats, I was convinced she would have been able to kill them all in a fierce battle. But there were dozens of these monsters... the only possible way to win would be through all out war between the Amank and the Stonecoats, and I knew the casualties would be far too great a cost. Something had to be done. I stood to my feet again, feeling none of the pain I'd expected to feel from the recently sutured wound in my stomach.

I turned to face Aeya, gently tracing her face with my hand and said what only a foolish love struck teenage boy could request.

"Give me the claw."

Chapter 18:

Faster Than Wind

"What? Are you crazy? I just stabbed you... you can't fight them." Aeya cried.

"You're right... I can't fight them. Neither can you. All I have to do is outrun them. I'm much faster than you are, especially since I hit you in the leg with the rock. If the stitches you gave me hold up, I'll be able to lead them away, maybe even lose them for good. You said there is a tunnel under the windmill right? I'll suit up, take the claw and run... stall them as long as you can."

"Please, let me do it. Have you lost faith in me already?"

"They've seen us up here. If you go and the townspeople can't account for you after the Stonecoats leave, they might figure out you're the Whoez. Give me the claw."

"No, Dominick." she glared at me.

"Now!" I barked with authority. She stood motionlessly and I took the claw from her hand and walked over to the mirror, where the Whoez was hiding in a flattened pile. I was practically stripped already, making it much easier and quicker to dress in the fine navy and gold attire. All at once, I'd become the very thing only a few hours earlier I was set out to kill. Who knew if now I'd actually succeed.

"Where is the tunnel?" I asked more gently. She pointed.

I charged into the tunnel claw in my fist, praying that my head start would be enough to come up with a plan. It wasn't very long before terrible gnashing sounds echoed from far off behind me. The tunnel ended at a pool of water. I took a deep breath and dove.

The water was very warm... much warmer than I'd anticipated. It must have been the vein of magma running within the nearby rock that kept the temperature so high. Luckily the path underwater was direct and well lit by the swimming Sabanora. Had it not been illuminated I would certainly have died from the extensively long passageway that lead to the surface. I popped up struggling to catch my breath after such a straining run and swim while the waves tossed me around between the two shores at the bottom of the canyon. I was at their mercy when I noticed the ruby stairs. Here it was... my chance. Only upward to go. I struggled to pull myself up onto the shore and made it up the first few steps before I collapsed. I was on my hands and knees panting hard... trying to do anything I could to catch my still lost lung full of air. The wind kicked up hard as if funneled into the valley between the cliff tops and all at once I caught my second breath. I began climbing as steady and as fast as I could. The rhythm of gasps between my steps overcame the pain and though my body was drained of all strength I progressed upward.

The water began to gurgle as Stonecoats bodies rose to the surface. The crowd had become much smaller than those who had overtaken the town. There were now roughly eight dark, wet bodies clawing over one another. I couldn't help but notice a few remained face down... and for a moment, I was proud that I had come as far as I had. The ones who survived the watery path were worse out of breath than I was but recovered in a fraction of the time.

Before I knew it, the six remaining had found their way to the stairs and began to climb several steps at a time. Given their lumbering, awkward bodies, I was certain they'd be at a disadvantage on the stairs, and yet, they ascended the stairs with far more grace and balance than I'd ever seen from them. The gap between us was closing in fast, as was the gap between me and the top of the ruby stairs. A sharp pain had been digging into my body, which I was certain was the puncture I'd suffered. I couldn't do it. Even if I made it to the top, the only way forward would be down. I had to make a last stand.

"BE STILL!" I shouted. I was shocked when they stopped. "This needs to end. I am not an Amank." I pulled off the mask to reveal strikingly different features than the monsters expected. They could see I was not an Amank by my pale skin and dark hair: A point I was glad that stuck. I reached into my undercoat pocket to press and relieve some of the sharp pressure on my wound, only to find a set of metal discs. I pulled one out and kept them in my hand. "If you leave me now, I won't kill you. I will leave this place and never war against your people again. You will all be seen as heroes for ridding the Whoez once and for all."

"WE WANT A BODY!" Their voices growled. Then the Stonecoats began inching towards me in a predatory stalk.

"I SAID BE STILL!" I commanded again and tossed a disc at the creatures as if I was skipping a stone on water. The motion nearly made me fall as the twist killed my balance. The disc missed wildly.

"That was a warning!" I shouted, hoping to further convince them I was still the skilled masked man they feared and that I was a force to be reckoned with. I unsheathed the sword on my hip, hoping to mirror the intimidating confidence Aeya had when she did it. "Hear me...When Piop died, the sky was dark. He was a friend and I take no joy in his death, but it was done in defense, not revenge."

"LIES!" They hissed. "What about the others?"

"There has been too much bloodshed... let it end now. Go and so will I." The words barely finished escaping when a Stonecoat lunged upward at me. The moment jolted me with adrenalin and without so much as a thought; I cut downward with the sword, embedding it into the space between the creature's neck and shoulder, nearly decapitating him. The body dropped onto the step just below my feet, twitched, and then fell taking my sword with it to the watery grave below. The other beasts watched their fallen comrade in horror as I kept their stare in my eyes, reaching into my pocket for more discs.

"Please... let it end." I said with sympathy on my breath. "I don't want to kill anymore. I just want to go."

In a wonderful turn of events, the ruby steps began to pull apart and rearrange. It was then I noticed the blood of the Stonecoat and remembered that I bled on the steps before they had sorted the last time. The platforms didn't change elevation but swam free in the air from one another. I had no idea why it would react in such a way, but I was grateful that the distraction occurred. The monsters clung to their steps and wobbled like a dog trying to stand in a moving car. The step I was standing on passed high over a group of steps in motion and in a reckless decision I jumped.

I fell far... past the monsters.... past the intended step... and down... until my overcoat became snagged on a much lower step, killing my momentum before tearing and allowing me to fall the rest of the way down into the water. The impact was like hitting cement and I sank. I struggled to surface, clawing at the Stonecoats bodies. When I broke the deep water and found the breath of air that was hiding, I grabbed on to the partially decapitated body, taking hold of my sword, still stuck partially in the torso, and floated. I stared up at the still moving steps, and the still frozen creatures. They were willing to fight and chase, but not to throw themselves to their death the way I had. So they began climbing down the stairs, which had not stopped sorting.

"IT'S OVER!" I shouted. "TELL YOUR PEOPLE THE WHOEZ IS DEAD. I WON'T COME BACK. LET THIS BE YOUR MOMENT TO BE A HERO!"

"WE NEED A BODY." the growled in poisoned defeat

"TAKE MY MASK, IT WILL HAVE TO DO. IT'S THE ONLY WAY TO END THE BLOODSHED. IF YOUR PEOPLE COME BACK, I WILL TOO." I yelled with deep authority and warning. It seemed to work. The creatures took their time to regroup and begin their descent. By then I had caught my breath and dove down into the water back towards the tunnel, all the while praying nothing was waiting for me on the other end.

I came up out of the water, tired and out of breath. I crawled the first few feet and then succumbed to the dizzying blur. A shadow marched towards me... It was Aeya.

Everything went black, and then suddenly I was falling. She caught me. I could hardly open my eyes.

"I need air." I moaned. She tore open the jacket and I gasped. Then in what felt like a moment of clarity I realized how the threshold worked. "There was light when I passed through the veil here but not when I came back. The common, missing element was the wind. Like the blurring wind from a raptured sprint, the wind rushed in when I journeyed between realities. I need wind to travel."

"Shhh, just take it easy. We only need to stay here for a while until the rest of the Stonecoats leave the town."

"No. I'm going home. Will you come with me?"

She didn't answer; instead, we held one another tightly. Suddenly, the tunnel filled with a spectral current; the glowing light grew, mixing with the wind, enshrouding us until I couldn't see Aeya in my arms anymore.

Reality was shattered... and in a moment, we were gone.

Chapter 19:

Home

The threshold passed with a sudden gust, leaving us once again outside. I was still suffering the injury of battle and horribly exhausted. I could barely make out the icy blue light of the coming dawn before losing consciousness. Aeya became frantic and shook me violently, it was still dark and to her, that meant something big was hungry. She did all she could to wake me and succeeded minutes later with a hard pulling of my hair.

"OW!" I shouted with all the attitude I'd give my mother for waking me up before noon on a Saturday."

What the heck!"

"It's dark!" she said with an unsettled tone. She was frozen in flexed preparation as though getting ready for battle.

"Did we make it back to my world?" The transition of worlds hadn't fully reached my comprehension and for a moment, I had no idea where I was.

"I don't know. It's... different." Aeya said, helping me to my feet. All at once I knew, I was home. We came through the threshold a mile or so away from my house, on the roof of a nearby fast food restaurant. I still didn't understand how these drop offs worked, but I was thankful we were close enough to home for me to recognize the location.

"Don't worry..." I assured her. "We're here." The dark is okay here. We took a few moments to rest, staring out over the concrete landscape lining the streets and surrounding us, as the early morning dawn peaked over the horizon like a brilliant golden lantern. The light poured over us and Aeya saw the sun for the first time. Watching her watch the golden wheel rise was a wonder I had never expected. As a child, you don't have the mental faculties to process the beauty of the sunrise, and by the time you are old enough to appreciate its splendor, the magic is lost by the familiarity of it. For Aeya, the sun was something brilliant and powerful, something she never expected and knew was beyond her. She stared with amazement as the colors and light bled through the early morning clouds, and I stared at her with swelled love for her newly discovered innocence, reigniting something that had been lost to me. I was excited to be done with the Whoez, excited to be back home, and excited to have her with me.

★★★★★

It was clear my parents didn't care much for Aeya. Somehow I didn't quite think my cover story through well enough. For one, I was hurt pretty badly. I was able to hide the stab wound in my gut, but my parents immediately noticed the giant claw scratch on my face. We made up some story about a wild dog attacking us. That was only the first of the lies my parents didn't accept that morning.

Aeya's Louisianna-ish accent was nearly all the proof my mother needed to conclude that this girl wasn't a foreigner but believed that she was in some kind of trouble. My dad thought she was a prostitute or sex slave or something of that nature but didn't come out and say it. Instead, he would fish for answers by asking 'Where did you meet?', 'Where are her parents?', 'Why can't she stay at her house?', 'Where were you staying for all those weeks if things were so bad?'. I had to hand it to my old man, he was no fool. I kept shrugging with my head down, saying "I don't know", which frustrated him even more. Aeya didn't look down at all. She had her head propped up proudly and kept staring kindly into my dad's eyes. I think her confidence only confused him more as he chewed on each word he attacked us with.

Somehow, despite the intense interrogation, my parents relented. Aeya was unfamiliar with enough of the simplest details of American culture that they couldn't validate their suspicions. So, despite their doubt, they allowed Aeya to stay at our house. For the time, she took my room and I slept in Tony's room. My dad took me aside and came down pretty hard on me.

"What the hell are you thinking? Do you have any idea what you are doing to your mother? You run away, not once but twice, and come home with some unkempt Asianish-Mexican... whatever she is."

"Don't be racist, dad!" I combated. I knew my dad wasn't racist, but the Italians have a smaller filter about political correctness, especially concerning race, and were hilariously touchy when being confronted about it. My hope was to deflect some of the anger and get him on a tangent.

"I don't care what she is…"

"Then why did you bring it up?" I asked smugly, proud that my plan was working.

"She could be black for all I care…" He said, pausing as he second-guessed her dark ethnicity. "… But you need to get your head on straight. I want a full game plan written up by the weekend. What are your relationship plans? Are you going to finish school? Is she going to go to school? Are you willing to quit football over her? Where is she going to live? If you plan on marrying her, how are you going to support her?"

"I don't know dad. I didn't think about it."

"That's the problem. You never think. I expect you to get your crap together."

"Yes, sir."

My dad stormed out of the room in anger. I never ended up giving him those answers.

★★★★★

The first few nights my mother patrolled the hallways to ensure we weren't bed hopping. I can't say I blame her because if she hadn't, I'm certain I would have found my way into my room. It must have been even more frustrating because Aeya's light never turned off as if she was always awake, ready to sneak off. Despite my mother's diligent sentry duty, patrolling the hall to prevent me from sneaking off with Aeya, some part of her must not have expected me to come out of my room. So when I left my room to use the restroom one night, she jolted as if being caught doing something she shouldn't. We hadn't spoken to one another much since the brief conversation when I came back. In fact, we hadn't really spoken much at all.

The air between my mother and I was silent. She knew there was nothing she could say to me after what she did but once she became regulated with medicine and therapy my dad kept insisting that I'd need to obey her and that she was still my mother. I resented him too when he had the nerve to force us together. Most times I'd just do the bare minimum and leave. Now, here we were crossing paths in the narrow hallway; me on my way to the restroom, her on her way nowhere. Our eyes met only briefly and before bouncing in endless directions in a desperate attempt to disconnect from one another. I was quickly drawn into the floral wallpaper, the only wallpaper in the house, which was outdated and yellowed but still somehow vibrant in my mind the way it was when I was younger. I remember my parents picking it out and playfully arguing over colors and designs, but everything seemed so playful then. I reached the bathroom which was no more than a few steps from where I passed my mother and as I grabbed the handle in a rush to escape the awkwardness of our passing, she spoke.

"Did you leave because of me?" she said reluctantly. I paused before opening the door and she continued unleashing mouthfuls of regret. "I'm so sorry Dominick. I tried... I know it doesn't seem like it, but I tried; I tried so hard. I understand why you hate me, but I want you to know I never stopped loving you. Even when..."

"Mom..." I interrupted with an unintentional sympathy. No sooner that I uttered the word "mom" did she lose composure and began sobbing without restraint and threw herself at my feet.

I wish I could say something. All those times I imagined the conversation with my mother, where she'd act so sad and hurt, and I would be tough and point out every single fault, every shameful thing she did, let her know how much I hated her, tell her how I wish she had died and occasionally told people at school that she had. I felt completely justified to remain bitter for the rest of my life... but for the first time, I didn't want to be. I saw my mom as a person; a very frail and broken mess who lived with possibly the deepest regret.

I reached down to her and tried bringing her to her feet, but she was weak and beyond operating her own functions. So rather than bringing her up to me, I knelt down with her and hugged her back. The embrace was hard gripped as if she was trying to push my body into hers. It wasn't angry, it was sweet. It was as though my heart had become overwhelmed and exploded, bringing breathlessness and pain in my chest, but it felt wonderful. I'm not sure when it happened, but I had forgiven her, it just took this long for us both to realize it.

"You haven't called me 'mom' in years." She said after a few moments of mutual weeping in our affectionate embrace.

I smiled at her with so much sympathy and regret of my own. Regret of how I treated her and the shame that even though I was a boy, she nearly killed me. I was overpowered by a girl to the point of death and there was nothing I could do about it. "I don't know why I left. I can't promise I won't leave again... but I can tell you this. If I leave again, it won't be because of anything you've done." I used my shirt to wipe the mess of tears from her face, consoling her. She smiled at me with a confused undeserving frown mixed in.

"I wanted to kill myself." She blurted out. "How could I live knowing what I almost did? What kind of mother tries to kill their child?" Those words 'what kind of mother tries to kill their child' had rolled through my mind daily since the event and now that she was the one to say it I knew the answer.

"For a long time, I wish you'd died. I wanted you to die before that day ever happened so I could go on thinking you loved me and never question how far your love would go." I admitted. "I never felt like that day ended; the fear, the anger, and the shame, it never went away. When I was hiding on the slide, I waited for you to come, certain you'd find me and try to kill me. What was scarier was that I was ready to kill you right back. Even after you were on your medicine for a while, I had a hard time sleeping. I wanted to forgive you, but I couldn't."

"I'm awful..." she confessed in a fit of sincere self-hatred.

"No, you were sick. You're better now." I assured her laying my hand on her shoulder. "Everything that happened, I'm ready to let it go."

She embraced me even harder and continued to weep. I don't know why but my mind drifted back as if recalling me to a specific event from years past that I'd long forgotten about... something so sad and yet, I remember it with fondness "Do you remember when grandpa died? You took time off work and stayed home with us all summer. I wanted to be sad because I missed grandpa, but I liked having you around. You'd sit and cry and I'd sit with you."

"I was an awful mess then too." She said, trying to piece together the point of one awful state with another.

"It wasn't perfect, but it wasn't all bad. You took us to the park and for walks. You let us play outside and occasionally take the blame when we'd get in trouble with dad. You were broken but still tried. After everything that happened between us, you still tried to make it better, which is more than I can say."

"Dominick, you didn't deserve what I did…"

"I know…. And you don't deserve what I did… You were sick when you hurt me but I wasn't sick for all these years I've been hurting you back." I said taking her hand. "Do you forgive me?" The words almost shocked me as they came from my mouth.

"Oh, Dom…" She said with an abundance of sympathy towards me, even more than I was giving her. She cried again and held me.

There was nothing more said about the incident between us, those many years ago. We both had learned to let go of what we couldn't change, rather than spending an eternity lost in a moment of shattered reality. I had forgiven my mother and she had forgiven me demonstrating the most uncomfortable truth of human nature that extends beyond all demographics; everyone wants to be forgiven.

Epilogue:
The New Mask

The night was hard for Aeya. She never got used the dark sky without being on permanent alert of the Stonecoats. It was even more difficult since no one in our world seemed to mind the dark anymore. Suburban life was a radical change from the community she knew, swarming with unfamiliar faces. I could tell she hated it. This world, which initially held many wonders to her, was changing her. Her shape bloated from the food, her demeanor became agitated, and her strong-willed nature had become lethargic.

Our days were spent almost entirely outside, walking, or hiking nearby trails. When night came, she would ensure she was indoors and comforted by the reassuring lights. The only time she seemed to enjoy my world was when we went running together. Then one day, without a word, she was gone...

I suspected that she might have traveled back into the Furtherland, so I climbed into the attic to confirm my suspicions. At first sight, all was just as it had been. The window was partially open, the mirror frame slightly askew, and no immediate signs of disruption were apparent. I don't know what I was expecting to find there. I turned and nearly went back downstairs when I became angry. She couldn't have just left. So I went over towards the mirror.

Behind the mirror-less frame, where we'd kept Nock's sword as it had been stored in the windmill, was a mask. At first I thought it was hers, a mask I hadn't seen since being chased up the Ruby stairs by the ferocious mountain devils, who were absolutely justified in wanting The Whoez dead. The ivory eggshell surrounded by fur and feathers, similar to the Whoez, but was not nearly as wild. Her egg shelled face plate was cracked and jagged, with full feathers jutting out like a lion's mane; showing her power and forceful nature. It suited her. This mask, my mask, was without feathers and restrained in width, but carved back at the top and sides, resembling hair pulled backward in a freezing run. Now my mask suited me.

I picked up the mask and turned it over to find a note with only two words. It was perhaps the sweetest and most endearing two words anyone could say to me, and it was written in such a fantastically innocent and flirty way that my heart actually swelled.

In beautifully clear penmanship, she wrote:
Catch Me...

I read those words over and over.

In those two words, I knew where she'd gone. I knew why she'd gone. She was homesick. Most importantly, in those two words, I knew she wanted me, loved and even needed me. How could I not chase her? In that moment, the entire adventure into the Furtherland crossed my mind. We'd been out for so long that her wild spirit was struggling to live a tamed life. The old woman said "Untamed things hurt on impulse."

She must have failed to realize that not all wild things are bad. Some wild impulses are driven by love... I saw this now. I knew I'd do the same thing. I'd chase Aeya, the Whoez, into the Furtherland and leave my family behind with all the pain and hurt I didn't plan to do.

I knew I couldn't explain to them where I'd be going and hardly had any strength to say a final goodbye. They would just have to assume that I'd run off with Aeya, which was true. My dad understood. After all, he knew that it was all about a girl.

I put on the mask she gave me, grabbed her father's sword and waited for the Furtherland to come and take me.

Once again reality was shattered... and I understood that while life appears to hold infinite possibilities... it is time that is limited. So chase what you want and run as fast as you can to get it.

J.D. Clair
AUTHOR

"Photo courtesy of Goodwill Industries of Southeastern Wisconsin, Inc. and John Grant Photography."

Son of the American Mid-West, J.D. Clair told offbeat stories that intrigued and frustrated his family and teachers. He was a loud mouthed trouble maker, whose passion for intricate narratives led to a deep affection for comics, theology, and mythology. This led to a Bachelors Degree in Creative Writing at the University of North Texas before returning to the Chicago suburbs where he lives with his wife and three children and participates in community charities.

Overweight, he killed himself by running, climbing stairs, and eating clean, which amounted to an 80 pound weight loss in a few months; during which the majority of "The Impossible Return to Innocence" was written. The story became a reflection of the physical transformation and documents various trials faced, including a loved one suffering a severe mental disorder.

"I learned dignity, self respect, and most difficult of all, that if you don't take yourself seriously, no one else will." - J.D. Clair

MERAKI HOUSE

P U B L I S H I N G

Publishing with
Soul, Creativity & Love

Meraki House Publishing, founded in 2015 has established its brand as an independent virtual publishing house designed to suit your needs as the Author, delivering the highest quality design, writing and editorial, publishing and marketing services to ensure your success.

"Where your needs as an Author have become ours as an independent Publishing House."

WWW.MERAKIHOUSE.COM

In partnership with
www.designisreborn.com

Copyright 2015, Meraki House Publishing

Marnie Kay, Founder & CEO
marniekay.com

UP NEXT by J.D Clair.....

Stonecoat
Due for release Fall 2016

Lightning Source UK Ltd.
Milton Keynes UK
UKOW01f2229060716

277812UK00002B/26/P